Sherlock Holmes
and the
Greyfriars School Mystery

By the same author

Sherlock Holmes and the Egyptian Hall Adventure
Sherlock Holmes and the Eminent Thespian
Sherlock Holmes and the Brighton Pavilion Mystery
Sherlock Holmes and the Houdini Birthright
Sherlock Holmes and the Man Who Lost Himself

Sherlock Holmes and the Greyfriars School Mystery

Val Andrews

**BREESE
BOOKS
LONDON**

First published by the author
in a limited edition in 1990

First published in this edition in 1997 by
Breese Books Ltd
164 Kensington Park Road, London W11 2ER, England

© Martin Breese, 1997

ISBN: 0 947533 55 9

Typeset in 11½/13½pt Caslon by
Ann Buchan (Typesetters), Middlesex
Printed and bound in Great Britain by
Itchen Printers Ltd, Southampton

Dedicated to the late Frank Richards.
His incredible output of brilliant school
stories gave many a working-class boy
a public-school education.

Introduction

Readers of some of my more recent accounts of the exploits of Mr Sherlock Holmes might almost be forgiven for thinking that he was involved in as many cases after his retirement as when he was in active practice. This is not really so, though I must admit that many of the matters investigated during his 'Indian Summer' were among the most intriguing.

Among these, 'The Greyfriars School Mystery' took me back to my old seat of learning and caused Holmes to neglect his bees yet again!

The events of this adventure took place in 1912 in 'The Garden of England'. It was a time when the world had not yet quite lost its sanity.

John H Watson, MD
October 1928

CHAPTER ONE

In the Beak's Lair

It was in the spring of 1912 that my old headmaster, Dr Locke of Greyfriars School in Kent (my own old seat of learning), wrote to enlist my aid concerning a missing manuscript. Of course I responded with a letter telling him that despite long association with my friend, Sherlock Holmes, I was not myself a detective. However, I could scarcely desert the old gentleman in his hour of need. Indeed I was delighted as well as amazed to learn that he was still in the land of the living, let alone still headmaster, and after some swift mental arithmetic I calculated his age to be at least eighty-five. I remembered thinking him extremely middle-aged when I had arrived at that school back in 1864 as an extremely scruffy twelve year old. I had emerged as head boy in 1870, but had not seen the good doctor since.

At his invitation I took the train to Courtfield Junction expecting to find everything at the school and in its vicinity to have changed out of all recognition. Instead my first visit to my old school in forty years was like a step back in time to rival anything contrived by H G Wells. As I entered the familiar gates it seemed as if my old chums Dobson, Smith and Carstairs Minor were punting a footer in the quad. Of course I knew that it could not be, for Dobson was a merchant banker; Smith, in spite of his age, was still in the army; whilst poor old Carstairs had died of typhoid fever when we were still at school. It could have been them though, it could have been, just as the fat youth with big spectacles, leaning against the wall, could have been 'Hippo' Craig, but was not. I noted that the short Eton-style jackets were still in use but the silk toppers of my day had been replaced by neat caps.

I peered into the doorway of the familiar tuck shop and espied what I took to be another ghost from the past. Instead, there was Mrs Mimble, much older yet unmistakable: no figuration of a nostalgic daydream she! The good dame looked me straight in the eye and with no display of surprise said, 'Master Watson . . . ain't seen you for a year or two, but you still owes me two shillin' for 'ot potatoes!' With trembling hand I paid her the two shillings and a further copper or two for a rock bun and a cup of her thick, strong, sweet tea. I sat at a chipped marble-topped table and although still bemused was alert enough to consult my watch to be sure that I still had a little time to spare before my appointment with Dr Locke.

As I sipped the sickly liquid of nostalgia and nibbled the crumbly flakes of blessed memory the stout lad, the one that had reminded me of 'Hippo' Craig, entered the tuck shop. He looked at me with complete lack of interest until, having searched his pockets and found only a bent French coin and an omnibus ticket, he threw me a calculating glance. After a longing look at the piles of cakes and vats of pop he blinked at me through his big spectacles and said, 'I say, sir, are you one of the paters? Your son and I are such chums you know!' Bemused, I replied, 'As you do not know which boy's pater I am, how can you be sure that the two of you are such chums?'

'Beast!'

'Eh?'

'Oh, I'm sorry, sir, I was referring to some other beast. What I really meant to say was that your son and I are sure to be chums because I am far and away the most popular chap at the school. Kindest friend and noblest foe you know!'

I said, 'Well it so happens that I am not one of the paters, but I am an old boy of the school here to see Dr Locke.'

He said, 'Oh well, I expect the two of you will have a good jaw. I get on splendidly with the Head you know, even if he is a bit of an old duffer. I say, I suppose you couldn't lend me five bob until my postal order comes?'

I gasped, 'Eh, what?'

He continued in glib fashion, 'You see I've been disappointed about a postal order from one of my titled relatives. Can't think what's holding it up. It's for seven and six, so if you'll lend me the five bob I'll give you the whole thing when it comes.' I have met a few confidence men in my time but never one so young or obviously practised. Like a hypnotized rabbit I handed two half-crowns to this fat weasel, yet venturing to ask, 'May I be permitted to know to whom I am lending this sum?'

'Eh? Oh, Bunter's the name, sir, of Bunter-Court in Surrey. My pater is a big man in the city, a bull or a bear or something, and he's not really a mean beast who never sends me any pocket money. Far from it and if you've heard anything else it's just those beasts, envious of a wealthy and popular fellow. I mean Wharton and his mob, scruffy crowd of hooligans, always trying to make out that my people are hard up and that Bunter-Court is really Bunter-Villa.' At this point an interval occurred during which Bunter, having passed most of my five shillings across Mrs Mimble's counter, consumed a huge pile of comestibles washing them down with huge draughts of ginger-beer. Then, after pausing for breath he continued, 'Oh yes, Wharton and his crowd even try to suggest that I'm fat you know! Of course I'm not a skinny ostrich like Toddy or Fishey, but just well covered as you can see.' Then he took his remaining few coppers from his pocket, looked at them, then looked thoughtfully at me. For one dreadful moment I thought he was going to stretch my generosity to breaking point. But doubtless catching the gleam in my eye he just nodded and rolled majestically out into the spring sunshine. I had to revise my first opinion of Master Bunter. His early display of shrewdity had been followed by a demonstration of stupidity that had been very hard to believe. Obviously this seemingly worldly but unintelligent boy was more to be pitied than blamed. As I left the tuck shop, Mrs Mimble called after me, 'You don't want to lend any money to Master Bunter . . . 'is postal orders never comes!' I nodded, smiled and waved to her as I left the shop, crossing the quad to enter the portals of my old seat of learning.

I knocked at the study door and a familiar voice bade me 'Enter!' There sat Dr Locke, exactly as I remembered him save for the mane of snow-white hair. He rose and I noted that despite his great age he was still lively of movement. He greeted me, 'Dr Watson, how nice of you to come. Pray do be seated.' I replied, 'Thank you, Doctor, but I think you had better call me Watson, as of yore.' He nodded benignly and said, 'As you wish, my dear Watson, and I am sure you realize that I would not have put you to this bother, were I not sorely troubled.' Before he reached the burden of his summoning me we spoke, I from uncertainty and he from politeness, of 'shoes and ships and sealing-wax and cabbages and kings', as befitted an academic and his scholar who had not seen each other for many years. Eventually, however, we got down to that which had caused him to bring me so far. Of course I knew that it was really the services of Sherlock Holmes that he was seeking, so I said, 'You do know, Dr Locke, that my friend has been retired from his occupation as a consulting detective for the better part of a decade? Keeps bees in Sussex you know!'

'But you keep in touch with him?' The tone of his enquiry was almost sharp.

'Why yes, and I visit him from time to time, but only on the rarest and most vital emergencies have I managed to tempt him to use his powers of deduction. Perhaps you could give me some idea of the problem which troubles you sir, for although not myself a detective Holmes's methods are known to me.'

'Quite so . . .' He hesitated and I could read the disappointment in his voice and his face at my failure to produce Sherlock Holmes. He continued, 'The problem concerns a manuscript, the property of the form-master of the Remove (as we still refer to the Lower Fourth) one Henry Samuel Quelch. He has mislaid, or (as he himself claims) been deprived of a work upon which he has been engaged for a very long time. You will not, I believe, remember Mr Quelch, as he did not join the staff until about the turn of the century. He is an able man, an MA, stern but just, which is of course a requirement for the form-master of the Remove.' When I enquired as to the nature of this manuscript which had been 'lost, stolen or strayed', Dr Locke said, 'It is a history of this school, a learned work requiring a great deal of research. Mr Quelch has laboured tirelessly upon it for at least ten years to my knowledge. All of his spare time is devoted to the task, evenings, half-holidays and even the sabbath!' The good doctor spoke without recrimination, for although he was a doctor of divinity he had always been broad of mind. In answer to my next question, concerning the possible existence of a copy of the manuscript, he said, 'Alas no, for who would expect a work of such limited interest to be purloined, and indeed what value could one put upon such a work save that which the author himself places upon it?'

I could picture, although I had not as yet clapped eyes upon him, the lonely school-master bowed over his desk and poring over innumerable foolscap sheets. Through his study window would waft the sounds of a world which he had chosen to forsake, at least each evening, half-holiday and Sunday. Undistracted by the cries of youthful voices, distant traffic and eventually the sounds of the night, I was reminded of my friend Sherlock Holmes who could at times display singleness of purpose when composing one of his famous monographs, or deep in the throes of a four-pipe problem. Such thoughts of Holmes reminded me to try and decide what he would have asked Dr Locke had he been present, so I enquired in what I hoped sounded like a business-like manner, 'You have not reported the matter to the police?'

Dr Locke pursed his lips and said, 'Mr Quelch is as anxious as I am to avoid such involvement lest it should lead to journalists making use of the incident. After all, such an incident if spoken of beyond these walls would not be exactly beneficial to a school for the sons of gentlemen!' I could quite see his point, for whilst no slur would attach to the wronged school-master engaged in a meritorious task, *any* publicity would be frowned upon by those who had entrusted offspring to the care of the secluded Kentish public school rather than to Harrow or Westminster.

'I have arranged for Mr Quelch to join us for tea. Both he and the repast should be here soon.' Dr Locke consulted his gold hunter before he continued, 'I am myself a trifle peckish and I'll wager, young Watson, that an eclair would soothe your own inner-man if memory serves me well!' His memory did serve him very well indeed, but forty years had dulled my own appetite for sweet confections. However, I just smiled politely as Mrs Kebble (rather like a cockney version of our own dear Mrs Hudson) served the tea and announced, 'Mr Quelch is 'ere, sir, a waitin' houtside!'

Henry Samuel Quelch proved to be a tall, gaunt, angular man of indeterminable age. He had the clean shaven face and neat mutton-chop side-burns of the typical school-master. More acidic than the benign Dr Locke, he was polite in a stern way. He nibbled at a cucumber sandwich whilst I tackled the chocolate eclair as manfully as I could. When Quelch told me that he had lost his manuscript but hours before Dr Locke had written to me I realized that his loss was, to him, of very great importance. He spoke earnestly, 'Dr Watson, my *History of*

Greyfriars will, when published, prove to be of outstanding interest to historians and scholars. That is if I regain it! I do not believe that I have energy or years enough left to begin the work again.'

In answer to my enquiry as to how near to completion the manuscript had been he said, 'Another three or four years of painstaking labour should see it finished, that is if I get it back.' Dr Locke said nothing at first but I read from his expression a certain disbelief in the reality of the work's eventual completion. Again he studied his watch and said, 'Mr Quelch, why do you not take Dr Watson to your study, the scene of the crime, eh what?' Then he turned a benign eye upon me and said, 'Oh yes, my dear Watson, I have followed your chronicles in the *Strand* with interest. Whilst at times I question your grammar I admit that they are agreeable to read.'

I bade farewell to Dr Locke, promising him that I would give Mr Quelch whatever help I could and accompanied the Remove master to his study. I remembered that apartment well from my own time as a Removite. In those days it had been the study of a Mr Spencer, a huge and terrifying man who had thrashed me with his ashplant in that very room many times. The bookcase still lined one wall and the sofa still stood exactly as it had been before the window, which gave a view of the quadrangle. I stood upon that same mat, upon which I had stood and quaked following the discovery of my involvement in some rag or jape.

Quelch opened the drawer from which his manuscript had evidently been taken. He explained to me that he had returned to his study and had sat at his desk to discover a junior boy of his class hiding behind the sofa. 'He had evidently hoped to remain undetected. When I asked him why he had come to my study he said that he had wanted to use the telephone.' (I noticed the instrument on the desk, an innovation unheard of at Greyfriars in my time.)

'I did not doubt this statement because I had caught this particular boy attempting to use my telephone on previous occasions. I punished him by giving him six with my cane, and considered the matter as closed. But soon after he had departed I discovered that my manuscript was missing.'

I asked if he would not have noticed that the boy walked out of his study with a heavy sheaf of papers. He said, 'Undoubtedly, I could scarcely have caned a boy with four hundred foolscap sheets concealed about his person without discovering them. I thought at first that he had hidden the papers somewhere within the study as a foolish prank. But I have searched the room over and over again without finding them.' I glanced at the window and enquired as to the possibility of the manuscript being disposed of through it, to someone else. Wearily, Quelch answered, 'Impossible, for the sash is broken and the window immovable. I have been waiting for Gosling, the porter, to repair it for weeks, with increasing impatience!' I tested the window and could not move it. Obviously a Greyfriars junior boy would have been even less able to open it. I said the obvious, 'Perhaps some other boy or person had been in your study earlier and that the boy you caned had nothing to do with the matter. Perhaps he is innocent of all save wanting to make use of your telephone.'

Then it was that Mr Quelch surprised me with the tone, one almost of hatred, in his voice. 'I try to be just, Dr Watson, but deep down in my heart I *know* that Vernon-Smith (for that is the name of the boy in question) is the culprit. Ever since he came to this school he has been a rebel. Oh, he does his school work well enough and is bright and intelligent, but he has a dislike of authority, of mine in particular. In return for his insolence I have punished him severely on many occasions. But however hard the beating, he has never cried out as other boys do. He is hard and cool beyond his years, not the right sort of boy for this school. His father has money, but it is not inherited wealth. Mr Vernon-Smith is in . . . business!' (He all but looked both ways before speaking the dreaded word!)

I must say that I was rather taken aback at this attitude in a school-master in this year of 1912, but simply said, 'What would this boy, this Vernon-Smith, *do* with your manuscript? Surely if he has stolen it there must be some motive?' My words seemed to annoy Mr Quelch. He said, 'His motive, sir, is to harm me! He is just not the sort of boy to benefit from a Greyfriars education. He may even destroy my manuscript or cast it to the winds. Who knows what may enter the mind of a boy of that kind?'

I suppose it was as much the thought of being able to prevent some possible miscarriage of justice as the importance or interest of the case that made me at that point determined to interest Holmes in it. I said, 'Mr Quelch, I will try and enlist my friend's aid in this matter. Despite the permanence of his retirement I feel sure that I will be able to gain his help.' Quelch was delighted, saying, 'Bless you, Dr Watson, I feel sure that your friend will quickly recognize a motive and method and bring Vernon-Smith to justice!' My motive was very different but I said nothing.

It was a fine evening and I decided to walk back to

Courtfield Station. I had not quite left behind the high walls of the school when I was surprised by the sudden appearance of a youth, landing upon the grass verge that edged the wall. Although he sported a rough tweed jacket he still wore the trousers of his school uniform and carried a scholar's satchel. As he picked himself up he was seemingly more concerned for the bag and its contents than for his own safety. He hitched it onto his shoulders and started to walk briskly in the direction of the main road. I did not know if he was aware of me, but I was certainly intrigued by his actions and his sudden appearance and most of all by the question in my mind concerning the contents of that school-bag. As far as I could remember from my own school days this was the time of evening when he should have been at prep, poring over books in his study. I considered that his bag might well contain the missing manuscript, so I followed him as casually as I could. The main road reached, he jumped onto an omnibus with a Courtfield destination board. I decided to mount the same vehicle to discover his destination. I wondered if I had stumbled upon the answer to the mystery of the missing *History of Greyfriars*. Perhaps I might recover the manuscript and absolve Vernon-Smith without having to trouble the Sussex bee-keeper!

The boy dismounted just before the town centre was reached. I did the same and again followed him as casually as I could. His pace slowed as we reached the Theatre Royal and to my surprise he made down a side-alley signposted Artiste's Entrance. My mind raced, considering the possibility that the lad was about to dispose of the manuscript to some theatrical producer, determined to dramatize it! Of course in retrospect *The History of Greyfriars* might not seem a highly valuable theatrical property, but I had no time to ponder such details. Deciding to take the bull by the horns I accosted the young man as he made to enter the stage-door.

I said, 'Look here, I know that you have broken bounds from Greyfriars. May I have your name and know what it is that you carry in your bag? By the way, I am a colleague of Sherlock Holmes!'

He whistled softly and said, 'My name is William Wibley, sir, of the Greyfriars Remove. It's a fair cop, as you detective johnnies say; though I would hardly have thought that a crime as minor as mine would interest a famous sleuth like jolly old Sherlock!' I spoke warmly, 'You consider the theft of an important manuscript as a trifle?' He started, 'Manuscript, what manuscript? Are you potty or what?' I considered this change of attitude on the part of one who had already all but owned up to be rather strange. I snapped, 'Let me see the contents of your bag!' He said, 'At this stage I suppose you might as well.'

He started to loosen the straps of his satchel and I began to congratulate myself upon my perception and prompt actions. I peered into the bag as he opened the flap. But instead of the bundle of foolscap that I expected, I found a japanned case, a cigar box and a bulky paper package. The case proved to contain cosmetic-materials, powder, spirit-gum and other theatrical accessories. The cigar-box revealed sticks of theatrical make-up, and the package held a wig! I asked him, 'What is the meaning of this? What are these theatrical requisites doing in a school-boy's satchel?'

Wibley breathed hard and said, 'I am an actor, sir, and was given the opportunity of playing a role in this professional production of *Hamlet*. My father is an actor, and as he owns his own theatre he just qualifies as a gentleman, so I am just about tolerated at the school. I founded the Remove Dramatic Society but of course that is not professional. However, this *is*, and I auditioned for the part of a page one half-holiday. I landed the part and of course the people here think I'm a local lad. It's not been easy breaking bounds and coming here each evening, then sneaking back in time for dorm, but so far I've managed not to be discovered. There are only a few more nights to run, but I suppose now the game is up and I might get the sack when you tell Quelch.'

Shaken by surprise I quickly regained my composure, saying, 'My dear boy, I owe you an apology. Your private affairs are no business of mine. I have, wrongly as it transpires, suspected you of implication in a quite different matter. I realize my mistake, so can only wish you theatrical success!'

Wibley blinked. 'You mean you are not going to give me away?'

The very idea! I said, 'Certainly not, I'm an old boy of Greyfriars, not a sneak!'

We shook hands and I made my way to the station. There, as I awaited my train, I pondered upon the episode. I said to myself, 'William Wibley, schoolboy and actor, Third Page in *Hamlet*. I can only admire such enterprise and ambition.'

CHAPTER TWO

Sherlock Holmes at Greyfriars

The following morning I wired Holmes that I would be coming to Fowlhaven. I knew that he would be pleased to see me, however crab-like his welcome. I had never quite understood why he had retired when barely fifty years old. Now, almost a decade later, his mind and body seemed as attuned as in those halcyon days when the game had been afoot.

'So Watson, you not only wish to lure me from my bees and settled life here to investigate some trifling matter, but you also wish me to go back to school! Surely the Courtfield police can deal with the matter of missing property?'

We were sitting on the chalk cliff, perhaps a mile from Holmes's cottage, and the bracing salt air was working wonders with my respiratory system. I had not breathed so easily for years and began to understand why Holmes had chosen to dwell there in retirement. We were in fact at the surviving edge of a long-disused chalk road, most of which had been claimed by the sea as the cliff had crumbled. Holmes was deeply interested in it. Changing the subject under discussion he said, 'The sea on this coast is quite relentless, Watson. This road was in use when we were small children. Within a decade this spot upon which we sit will have been claimed by the ocean. As soon as the end of this present century my cottage may be threatened, though it will not trouble me.'

I ventured, 'I wonder how far out to sea the land here once stretched?' He replied, 'As far as what we now call France. There was once a town about three miles out there.' He gestured towards the wildly flowing ocean with the stem of a familiar clay. 'It is still there in fact and sometimes when the wind and waves are behaving in a certain way the bells of the engulfed church can be heard.' He picked up a chalk-encrusted horse shoe from what remained of the track and studied it. 'Amazing to think that such a heavy vehicle could have been driven once where no road survives.' I looked at the horse shoe and ventured to say, 'How can you tell what size the vehicle was from the shoe of the horse that pulled it, and indeed how can you be sure that the horse was not ridden rather than driven?' He replied, 'By its size, Watson, it belongs to a draught horse. Is it a Shire . . . no, a Clydesdale I think . . . see how deep it is, characteristic of shoes fitted to that breed. The vehicle would have been making slow progress when the shoe was cast.' I said, warmly, 'Oh come, Holmes, you jest! Even your methods could not estimate the speed of a vehicle, forty years ago, on a now non-existent chalk track!' He smiled his old familiar smile of satisfaction at a puzzle presented and solved. 'The horse was lame, for see how the farrier had driven one of the nails at the wrong angle. If the horse had walked that long on this shoe he would have been slow indeed.'

There was nothing more I could say to this so we just sat and smoked in silence for a few minutes. Then Holmes spoke.

'Watson, this business of Mr Quelch's missing manuscript intrigues me. I can well understand how a man who has spent ten years labouring upon it would be so anxious for its return. But what value could such a work have for anyone else. Come, you are a man of letters Watson, and as such you must know that *The History of Greyfriars* is a subject of purely parochial interest. The author of such a work, far from fighting off publishers' offers, may well end up paying for its issue himself. Such works are known in the trade as vanity publications, are they not? As for the suspect, this boy Vernon-Smith may be vindictive enough to have deprived Quelch of his manuscript, but why has he not made his move? He has not returned it secretly in mutilated condition, nor written some gloating note in disguised handwriting or demanded some ransom for its safe return. Any of these things I could understand, but I feel that a boy intent upon making his school-master suffer would have played his cards by now.'

I said nothing, for I dared not break the spell which I felt had been cast upon Holmes; from what source I knew not but thanked my Maker for it. Holmes worked furiously on his pipe, then after what seemed like an age he said, 'We will go to Greyfriars, Watson, you and I, to see what we can discover. However, I do not wish my sleep to be disturbed by the antics of unruly boys, so we will put up at a hostelry in the vicinity.'

That evening we dined at Sir Harry Preston's in Brighton and Holmes for this expedition discarded his country farmer down on his luck disguise and we both arrived at the hotel as if we were dining at Simpson's. The trout was good, as was the mousse. The waiters hovered around us and performed their work with professional skill. One of them I thought to be Italian but Holmes pronounced him Corsican, and enquiry proved him correct. As we savoured our brandies after the meal I thanked Holmes for his promise to investigate the matter of the missing *History of Greyfriars*. He said, 'Watson, it would be a poor thing if I were not able to help a chum to keep a promise to the head of his old school.' I said nothing, for my heart was too full. Although Holmes had once referred to me as his only friend I preferred his use of the word chum. He was the best and wisest man I had ever known, apart from which I felt that he was, in schoolboy parlance, an absolute brick.

I wondered what my friend would make of Greyfriars, for I knew that he was himself a product of the English public-school system, though he seldom mentioned his schooldays. He had little interest in organized sports and games aside from boxing and fencing, so I could not imagine him as a popular chap at such an institution where his interest in science and languages would have branded him a swot.

The following morning we took a cab to Lewes and from there a train to Tonbridge. There followed a series of short, sharp journeys by rail until we gained Courtfield Junction. Holmes muttered to the effect that we would have done better to go to Charing Cross and take a direct train from there. As it happened he was right as far as the time taken was concerned. Then from Courtfield Junction we took an ancient horse-drawn cab complete with elderly horse and even more elderly driver. The cabby touched his hat and asked, 'Where to, gents?' Holmes asked him, 'Can you recommend a hostelry where we might stay, in the general proximity of Greyfriars School?' He looked at us craftily and said, ' 'Ere for the Wapshot races eh, gents? The Cross Keys would sootcher, I reckon. Much patronized by the racing fraternity it is, punters and bookies alike. As for its promiskety to the big school, well one or two of them young rips could tell yer 'ow close it is!'

I was at the point of protest but Holmes gave me a silencing glare. He said, 'The Cross Keys it is then, driver, but don't hurry that poor beast.' Inside the cab he said, 'Watson, the racing fraternity are far more interesting than the usual collection of commercial travellers.'

We arrived surprisingly quickly at the Cross Keys and having reached it I remembered the place well, having once got six on the bags from old Spencer for breaking bounds to visit it. I went there but once, but the more daring sparks used to go there frequently to bet on horses and play nap. Yes and some of them even for a dash of whisky in their ginger-beer; such fellows were referred to as cads.

The rooms that we were offered at the inn looked comfortable enough, but the landlord could not resist romancing as to the style of his clientele. 'These 'ere two connecting rooms 'as just been vacated by Lord Derby and 'is valet!' Holmes examined the two rooms swiftly and said, 'On the contrary. These rooms were last occupied by a man with the initials H S and his mistress, a woman with artificially coloured red hair.' The landlord stood open mouthed as Holmes continued, 'I note that you have allowed your maids to simply tidy the bedclothes rather than changing them. Otherwise I would not have found an extremely long hennaed hair, and a cuff-link bearing the initials H S.' I could not resist asking, 'How do you know that she was his mistress rather than his wife or niece, for instance?' Holmes explained, 'A husband and wife would be far more likely to occupy a double room. Had the lady been a niece, secretary or other relative or employee I doubt if the carpet betwixt his bed and the connecting door would bear so many fresh female foot tracks! A tall woman, with size six boots and weighing about nine stone and four pounds. Landlord, kindly see to it that the sheets and pillows are changed!'

Outside the inn we stood upon the towpath and watched the sparkling waters of the Sark rush by. Holmes said, 'Upon my word, Watson, you never did tell me that your old school was in such splendid surroundings!' I said, 'One never thinks of one's good fortune when it is unravelling. Who would have thought, for example, that we would look back on the old days when we shared the rooms at Baker Street as halcyon ones? I certainly knew that those days were the happiest of my life.'

Later we walked to the school, just a short stroll along the towpath. No sooner had we entered the gates than I suffered the indignity of having my hat knocked off by a missive which turned out to be a cricket ball. Fond as I am of the sound of leather on willow, that of leather on felt pleases me not at all. Picking up my dented billycock I ruefully rubbed it on my sleeve. Gosling, the school porter, who had seemed like an ancient monument in my day, now seemed like Methuselah of old. He said, 'Very sorry, sir, begging your parding but it's always 'appenin'. It's what comes of 'avin' boys abaht. What I says is this 'ere . . . all boys is rips!' Then, gazing intently into my face he said, ' 'Ere, I remember you! Young Watkins ain't it?' I corrected him, 'Watson!' He continued, 'Yus, that's right, Watkins. Made you 'ead boy didn't they . . . though I can't imagine why. Made yer way in the world 'ave yer?' I told him that I had been, in turns, a soldier, a doctor and a writer. He said, 'Never mind. We can't all be George Robey, eh?' As Holmes turned a chuckle into a cough he attracted Gosling's attention. ' 'Oo's this 'ere, then?' When I told him 'Sherlock Holmes', he told me to 'Pull the other leg, it's got bells on!'

Suddenly we were surrounded by five junior schoolboys. Fresh faced, they raised their caps smartly.

'I say, sir, I'm frightfully sorry. Didn't mean to nut you with the jolly old ball!'

'Rather not!'

'Sorry, sir!'

'Jolly sorry!'

'The sorrowfulness is terrific esteemed and ludicrous, sir!'

The last remark came from a dusky-faced youth, evidently from the East Indies. Another of the lads shot a shrewd glance at my friend and asked him, 'I say, sir, aren't you Sherlock Holmes, the jolly old sleuth from Baker Street?' Holmes bowed in courtly manner and said, 'The very same, at your service gentlemen.'

One of the boys, who introduced himself as Bob Cherry, said, 'I say, sir, that was a jolly exciting case in the Christmas *Strand*, the one about Lady Frances Carfax!' This was Holmes's opportunity to gesture towards me and say, 'Please

meet my friend, colleague and Boswell, Dr John Watson.'
Although I was not quite such a success as Holmes, the
boys were uncommonly civil towards me. They told us they
were Wharton, Cherry, Bull, Nugent and Hurree Singh. It
was Wharton who was their spokesman. 'They call us the
Famous Five and we are having a bit of a feed in number
one study this evening. You know, a few sosses and some
pop. I suppose, Mr Holmes, yourself and Dr Watson would
not care to join us . . . we'd be honoured, wouldn't we
chaps?'

'Hear, hear!'

'Honoured!'

'Jolly honoured!'

'The honouredfulness would be terrific!'

To my amazement Holmes accepted the invitation with
good grace, obliging us to visit Remove study number one
at six of the clock. The Removites cheered us as we went on
our way and entered the main building which formed part
of a quartet which was collectively Greyfriars School. Holmes
assured me that the building was a restoration of a Norman
original. 'Probably a monastery, burned down by King Hal
and later rebuilt.'

As our footsteps led us in the direction of masters' studies we passed the half-open door of the Masters' Common-room. Conversation, lively though not cheerful, fil-
tered out, and I could not resist looking in to see if any
staff member from my day survived. They introduced
themselves, Capper, Lascelles, Wigg, Carpentier . . . all
were new faces to me. Then I espied the portly figure of
Mr Prout who had been my form-master when I was in
the Fifth. He was of course considerably older, but his
shadow had grown no less. He treated us to a monologue

concerning the stupidity of the modern boy as opposed to those of a decade or two ago. Then all the masters competed to name the most stupid boy in the school. Each claimed that his particular form held the prize-winner. Prout claimed Coker of the Fifth, but all morosely agreed in the end that they could not beat Bunter of the Remove.

Evidently the fat boy's spelling, mathematical incompetence and untruthfulness were as legendary as his actual stupidity. When I introduced Holmes to the masters I was surprised to learn that the loss of Quelch's manuscript was no longer a secret, at least from the staff. They were not backward in putting two and two together regarding a visit from Sherlock Holmes. That *The History of Greyfriars* was twaddle seemed to be the general view, one master even voicing the opinion that it was a task designed to get its author off some of his staff duties!

As we continued towards our goal Holmes turned to me and said, 'Well, Watson, there seems to be little love lost between Mr Quelch and his colleagues. Now if we were not men of science you could say that we already had four or five good, strong suspects concerning the theft of *The History of Greyfriars*.

I took Holmes first to see Dr Locke who was absolutely delighted that I had actually produced the great detective. He said, 'Watson, when you were head-boy I could always rely upon you, and obviously I still may!' Then, turning to Holmes, he said, 'My dear Mr Holmes, I cannot tell you how glad I am that the matter of Mr Quelch's missing *History* is in your capable hands, for his sake and the sake of the school.' Holmes replied, 'Dr Locke, I cannot guarantee to solve the problem but if I do not it will not be for want of trying.' Then he turned to me saying, 'Now,

Watson, let us begin the investigation. For remember, we have an appointment at six!' I offered up a silent prayer that Holmes would not divulge the nature of our appointment in a Remove study, and my prayer was answered.

Our next stop was at Mr Quelch's study where the Remove master was delighted to welcome my friend. Holmes could have learned little more than I had from his examination of the study, but I felt sure that his keen glances and use of his lens inspired confidence in Mr Quelch. Holmes asked some rather pointed questions.

'This Vernon-Smith, have you had occasion to punish him often since he has been in your form?'

'Often, yes, quite often.'

'And has he ever taken what might be termed revenge?'

'Why no, he is just . . . insolent.'

'Insolent in what manner?'

'When caned severely he affects not to feel pain.'

'I see . . .' Holmes considered deeply. 'Unless he is far deeper than one would suppose it seems unlikely that he would suddenly decide to take revenge. And could it not be, Mr Quelch, that he tries to accept punishment as an inevitable part of life's pattern?'

'You are defending this boy?' Quelch coloured slightly. Holmes's eyes narrowed almost imperceptibly. 'How can I defend someone that I have never even met? But if you would have the goodness to summon him here, Mr Quelch, I would like to question him.' The school-master opened the study door and peered out. Then he rapped loudly, in an acid voice, 'Fish! Find Vernon-Smith and tell him to come to my study at once. Go on, quickly boy!' There was an answering 'Yes, sir!' and a patter of fast retreating feet. Holmes resumed his questions.

'Is Vernon-Smith a good scholar?'

'Quite good, yes, but . . .'

'Is he good at sports and games?'

'Why yes, I believe he is . . .'

'What, then, are these wrongs for which you have had to so severely punish him?'

'Smoking, breaking bounds, gambling . . .'

'He is the only boy in your form guilty of these misdeeds?'

'No . . . there are others . . . but . . .'

'I see, and you punish these others just as severely as you do Vernon-Smith? I hardly need to have your answer to that question do I, Mr Quelch, for I have heard that you are a just man. Stern, but just.'

Quelch breathed long and hard before he replied. 'Mr Holmes, it is not normal for a fourteen-year-old boy to be able to resist the urge to cry out when severely caned. No other boy in my care has ever been able to do so. He will not allow me the satisfaction of knowing that he has been hurt. He is a bad hat, as I think you will agree when you have spoken with him.'

Holmes said, 'I look forward to doing so.' He had, I felt, struck a raw nerve in Mr Quelch. There was a tap on the door and the junior, Fish, who had been sent to summon Vernon-Smith, stood nervously before his form master. To my surprise I soon realized that he was an American youngster. He was tall, gaunt and wore huge horn-rimmed spectacles. He said, 'Say, Mr Quelch, sir, that pesky geek Smithy, he ain't in the joint any place!' Quelch, giving us a skyward glance, breathed the word 'American!' Then said to the boy, 'Fish, pray express yourself in English. You say that Vernon-Smith cannot be found?' Fish replied, 'Yes, sir! Why that pie-can just ain't around, I'll tell a man, I've looked everywhere!' As Fish retreated from the room Mr Quelch said to us, 'His father is an American financier you know. The governors of the school have evidently much to thank him for, so he could hardly be turned away.' I could not help but ask, 'Is his father even wealthier than Vernon-Smith's?' I could have bitten my tongue as soon as I had spoken, but Holmes rescued me by saying, 'Come, Watson, there is nothing to be gained from a pursuance of this subject. Let us leave Mr Quelch in peace for the moment. Remember we have an appointment to keep.'

'What ho, make room for the jolly old sleuth and his Boswell, you fellows!' Gladly we crammed ourselves into the already crowded Remove study. Room was made for us on the sofa which was minus most of its stuffing, and the cheery Removites perched, sat or leant as best they could. I recognized the five youngsters that we had met earlier, but quite a few more were present. Several stone bottles of ginger-beer were produced and we were given a glass each, but the others had to make do with cracked cups, tins, and the slop basin from a tea set with which Hurree Singh had to make do. I had not tasted the gassy, spicy liquid in forty years, and soon realized why! Yet Holmes seemed almost to enjoy it.

'A toast!'

'Rather, a jolly old toast! Who shall propose it? How about you, Inky?'

So it fell to the lot of the dusky junior to raise his slop basin and make the speech.

'I raise my chalice in toastfulness to the esteemed and

honourable detective and his ludicrous chum . . . that is, esteemed colleague!'

The boys as ever were amused by the quaint style of speech adopted by their dusky chum. But Holmes looked thoughtful as he said, 'Master Singh, that is your name, is it not?'

'Ratherfully esteemed, sir, Hurree Jamset Ram Singh.'

'You are from the Indian province of Bhanaphur, are you not?'

'Indeedfully, yes, sir, but howfully did you know?'

Holmes explained, 'There was a period in my life, lasting for several years, when everyone believed me dead, Watson included. But for part of that time I was at a monastery in Bhanaphur, studying with the monks.'

Bob Cherry asked, 'You mean you recognized old Inky's funny old way of talking, sir?'

'Yes, he speaks exactly as the monks do. In that part of the world it is the style of English used by the highest caste.'

Hurree Singh bowed and placed the palms of his hands together, saying, 'I am their nabob, sir, and one day I will rule that land.'

Next came sausages, and there should also have been some buns, but it was generally considered that the fat lad, Bunter, had snaffled the lot. A search was made for Bunter, but he could not be found. When I asked the boys how they could be so sure that Bunter was the culprit I was told, 'Whenever any grub is missing it is always our resident porpoise that has nabbed it!' Holmes remarked, 'Ah, that our work had always been so easy, eh Watson?'

We stayed for the better part of an hour, disturbed only by the visit of some sixth-form prefects who were searching for Vernon Smith. Wharton remarked, with concern, 'Old Smithy will get the sack for sure this time. Though if he were to turn up now, the Head just might let him off with a whopping.'

Before we left the school we learned that an extensive search had revealed no sign of Vernon-Smith, but a prefect, on looking into the box-room, had discovered Bunter engaged in the demolition of a huge bag of buns!

We strolled back to the Cross Keys and in its cool bar parlour sampled old ale from pewter tankards. I remarked to Holmes that it was an improvement upon the beverage that we had supped in Wharton's study. He said, 'Yes, but the spirit in which it was given pleased me, Watson, and yourself too, I'll be bound.' Then he was silent and thoughtful for some minutes before asking me, 'What do you make of Mr Quelch?' I replied, 'I think he is a worried man and troubled by more than the loss of his manuscript.' Holmes agreed, saying, 'The feud that he has with Vernon-Smith troubles him deeply. He is like a man who beats his disobedient dog, then finding that it does not yelp knows not what to do. He is ashamed, yet dare not let the beast beat him.' Then, before we turned in, he added, 'I am far more concerned now for the well-being of young Smith than I am about Quelch's *History of Greyfriars*.' I was glad that my friend had reached a similar conclusion to my own.

CHAPTER THREE

Inspector Grimes
Pays a Call

Breakfast at the Cross Keys was a very different experience to a similar repast at Baker Street or Fowlhaven. In rural England at that time they still tended to make rather more of the first meal of the day. Sausages and mash in such quantity struck me as being more suitable for luncheon or high tea. I remarked as much to Holmes. The detective smiled wryly and said, 'My dear Watson, these particular sausages have featured at both high tea and breakfast. Refused last evening by some person of small appetite they have made a game reappearance for our benefit this morning!'

I looked at my sausages with renewed interest, saying, 'You mean that you suspect that the landlord has fobbed us off with a warmed-up breakfast?' Holmes replied, 'It is obvious, Watson, to the keen observer. When you cook a sausage you throw it either onto a hot plate or into a pan of hot fat. When it has been cooked for a prescribed time it is turned over and when both sides have been cooked the sausage is removed. Now whilst the cooking affects the whole sausage, those portions of it which come into actual contact with the pan or plate are darker, forming a line or scar. To fully cook it you could produce only two such lines, but these sausages, my dear Doctor, have each four such marks denoting that they have been twice cooked. As they are made largely of pork you will, as a medical man, be fully aware of the dangers involved. I for one will refuse to accept them!'

The landlord replaced our sausage and mash with plates of bacon and egg with bad grace, denying Holmes's accusation. But his manner was furtive and I could see that Holmes's deductions had been accurate! With equally bad grace our host jerked a thumb in the direction of the bar parlour, saying, 'Police inspector wants to see yer!'

The parlour was as yet unoccupied except by a burly man of military style who introduced himself as Inspector Grimes, Courtfield Constabulary. I wondered if perhaps Mr Quelch had been unable to keep his problem a secret any longer, but evidently it was another matter that had prompted the visit.

'Last night, Mr Holmes, a Courtfield jeweller was not only robbed but actually murdered. We haven't had a murder in Courtfield since before my time, and I've been here thirty years. The coincidental visit of a celebrated detective seemed to me like providence!'

Holmes smiled kindly, saying, 'Come, Inspector, if you have had a hand on the local pulse for three decades I'll wager that you are more than competent to handle the situation. Dr Watson and I are staying at Courtfield for a few days' holiday. I am, you may have heard, retired completely from criminology.' At this the policeman's face fell. He said, 'I was hoping against hope that you would give me a hand, retired or no. I'll do all the donkey work, or my men will!' I was intrigued enough to say, 'Come, Holmes, it could do no harm . . .' Perhaps Holmes felt that fate had taken a hand somewhere along the line, as I did. He said, 'Oh very well . . . but you have Dr Watson to thank for my participation, Inspector. Now, shall we start with the scene of the crime?'

The delighted Grimes led us from the hostelry to the large limousine which stood outside. Holmes regarded the motor car with interest, remarking to me, 'A little different from the growler that Lestrade had to rattle about in, eh Watson? But not quite as reliable, though, I see.' I asked, 'In what way?' He replied, 'The vehicle is patently a new one, yet one of its wheels has already been replaced.' It was true, and indeed the damaged wheel could be seen, attached to the back of the car. The inspector smiled indulgently at this rather elementary deduction. But then Holmes, almost as if he felt that some demonstration were required of him, remarked, 'I trust you enjoyed the vacation from which you have but recently returned, Inspector? I notice that the weather was bracing rather than warm; I am rather fond of Margate myself! Your wife evidently likes the resort too, enough to decide to stay there for a few days longer. This must be making life difficult for you at home, with your housemaid being also on holiday!'

Grimes stood, holding the car door open but making no other movement. He looked as if he had been turned to stone at a moment of great astonishment. After what seemed like an age, he gasped, 'Bless my soul!' Then a glimmering of mistaken understanding crossed his mind and showed in his honest, open face. He said, 'You have recently been there yourself and caught sight of me?' Holmes chuckled, 'I have not been to Margate for many years, Inspector, but as the conjurer says, it's easy when you know how! That you have recently been exposed to a more bracing climate than occurred locally is obvious. You have wind burn rather than sun tan.'

I interrupted, 'Could the inspector not have been thus affected at Brighton or Worthing?' The detective said, 'Possibly, but it was not so. You see he has two omnibus tickets, issued by a company in Margate (for I recognize the style of print and the paper texture) folded to become small and inserted into the band of his hat. It is the habit of many men to lodge their tickets thus, against the require-ment of inspection.'

Grimes smiled, 'I see. But wait a minute, how could you possibly know that my wife has decided to stay on in Margate and that the servant girl does not return until next Monday?'

Holmes explained, 'Had your wife or the girl been at your home, one or other of them would most certainly have noticed the tickets and removed them when brushing your hat. Indeed it would only have been a matter of time before you noticed them and removed them yourself, suggesting a very recent return.'

The inspector rounded on his sergeant who sat at the wheel of the car. 'Reynolds, you should have noticed that I was walking around with bus tickets in my hat band! You'll never make a detective if you don't observe!'

As we sank back into the comfort of the back seats of the big car I considered that Grimes had been wise to enlist the aid of my friend, who although retired had lost none of his mental agility. Although the short drive was a smooth one I knew that Holmes would have preferred the noise and rattle of a hansom. He had always enjoyed the open nature of such a cab. After a few minutes we pulled up outside a jeweller's shop with H Silverman emblazoned upon its façade. It was next to a large double-fronted shop, or rather café, through the clear windows of which could be seen tables at which sat patrons, being waited upon by a stout, elderly gentleman wearing a skull cap. Grimes muttered, 'That's Uncle Clegg. He's a local character. Hates the boys from the big school despite the fact that they provide him with most of his takings.' Holmes enquired, 'Have you asked this Uncle Clegg if he saw anything unusual last night?' Grimes said, 'I have indeed, sir, but as it was a half-holiday at Greyfriars he had the usual bunfight to contend with. Evidently he had some trouble with a fat lad, Bunter, who consumed a great deal and was then unable to pay! Some of his school fellows had to settle his bill, but they were not too happy about it.' Holmes said, 'That would have been quite early in the evening. Bunter was apprehended in the school box-room at about six-thirty or so, consuming a large bag of buns. Really, his capacity for foodstuffs appears to be phenomenal.' Having been one of Bunter's victims but a day or two earlier, I could only agree!

Outside the jeweller's a uniformed constable stood on guard, and saluted smartly as we neared the entrance door. The constable shot a shrewd glance at Holmes and said to Grimes, 'Nothing to report, Inspector, except that a chap from the *Courtfield Gazette* wanted to go in. I sent him off with a flea in his ear!'

The shop's interior was rather typical of such places, with a lining of glass cases filled with rings, watches, bracelets and necklaces. An ugly crimson stain on a mat which was spread in front of the counter told much of the story. Grimes filled in the details. 'Mr Silverman was shot in the chest with a single bullet fired from a rifle. When we discovered him he was still alive, but he did not regain consciousness and died within the hour.'

Holmes asked, 'Who found him?'

Grimes replied, 'A neighbouring shopkeeper, a draper who was working late, sprucing up his shop for the morrow. He heard a noise suggestive of a disagreement at about nine of the clock. He was surprised because old Silverman was usually off his premises by that time. The intruder had gone by the time the draper came on to the scene, and the door had been left wide open.'

Holmes examined the door. 'No sign of force so the intruder was admitted, or had a key, unless he picked the lock.' He studied the lock with his lens. 'Picked with a curved wire . . . evidently he was a practised burglar.'

I asked a rather mundane question. 'What did the intruder take, Inspector, for the shop seems little disturbed?' Grimes replied, 'According to Mrs Silverman there are only three or four pieces missing, but they are the most valuable items in the shop. For example, an antique gold watch and an all but priceless pearl necklace.'

Sherlock Holmes, by this time squatting near the blood-stained mat, asked, 'I assume you have studied any footprints?' Grimes said, 'Yes, sir, but there are so many. It is a busy shop.' In reply to Holmes's enquiry regarding strange substances he said, 'None other than those that one would expect to find in this part of Kent; chalk, leaves, stuff like that.'

Holmes had taken a scrap of stiff paper from his wallet and was working it along the floor near the mat. He raised it to reveal some rather minute pieces of vegetation. He studied them with his lens, then handed both paper and glass to the inspector. 'Take a look, Grimes. What do you make of that?' The burly police inspector moved the lens to and fro as if unused to the practice. He said, 'Some sort of grass or weed, which could have been trodden in from almost anywhere in a rural community.' Much the same thought had occurred to me but I could see that Holmes did not dismiss the tiny green fragments so easily. He said, 'Not grass or weeds, but pieces of a water plant from a very distinctive species.' Grimes shrugged, 'The Sark flows only a few hundred yards from here.' Holmes nodded. 'It's a fast-moving trout stream and not the ideal place for a plant of this variety. This particular sub-species grows only in the antipodes to my knowledge. I suppose it might survive here in some quiet swamp or secluded watery clump. Tell me, Inspector, are there any naturalists residing in this area?'

Grimes pondered, then said, 'Sir Hilton Popper! He brought a lot of foreign flora and fauna back from his travels. In fact I had to remonstrate with him for introducing Canadian grey squirrels onto his estate. The little blighters have spread all over the district and they do a lot of damage. I told him that I didn't mind his black swans or golden pheasants, but those little grey blighters are vermin!'

Holmes brightened. 'He has black swans, eh? Tell me, does he keep them on his estate?'

'No, sir, on his island. He's got a sort of pond there, enclosed by thick bushes . . .'

'He owns an island?' Holmes was interested now.

'Why, yes. Popper's Island is in the middle of a wide reach of the Sark, quite near to the big school. In fact, Sir Hilton is forever complaining to me of the young rips trespassing on his island.'

I could not resist interjecting, 'Mark Twain has much to answer for!' Both Holmes and Grimes fixed me with gimlet glares. Grimes said nothing, but Holmes snapped, 'Really, Watson, please do not allow *Tom Sawyer* and *Huckleberry Finn* to cloud the issue!' I lapsed into silence.

Holmes examined the blood-stained mat again, the bullet which had caused the death of the jeweller, and everything in the shop which could possibly have any bearing on the crime. Then he settled upon a stool behind the glass-topped counter on which he rested an elbow and settled his head in his hand. It was rather as if had gone into a trance, from which none of us dared to distract him. Then after what seemed like an hour but was in fact less than five minutes, Holmes roused himself and said to Grimes, 'I suppose some person treading some exotic weed into the shop may have no bearing on this affair. I can only wish that Silverman had cleaned, swept or washed the floor just before this terrible event occurred, for if he had we would know that footprints and other signs would have been caused either by himself or the intruder. But obviously he did not, and we can only hope that this one spark of possible light is not a false trail.'

Grimes said, 'I have nothing better to go on, so I'm game to follow any trail!'

Holmes leapt down from his stool and said, 'Good man,

Inspector, so long as you do realize that it could be a wild-goose chase.' (I was tempted to say 'Or black swan chase!' but I wisely resisted the temptation.)

We emerged once more into the spring sunlight and clambered into the big limousine. Grimes leant forward to instruct his sergeant. 'Popper's Island, Reynolds, or as near to it as you can get the car.' Five minutes later, having crossed a bridge, Reynolds pulled the car over onto a piece of waste ground. He turned and said, 'As near as I can go, sir. It's the towpath from here on.' Grimes said, 'You can take the car back to the station, Reynolds, for we will be here for a while. I suggest that you return for us in about two hours. Will that be long enough, Mr Holmes?'

The detective was filling a bulldog pipe from his pouch. He said, 'If not, it will mean that we are on the wrong trail.' He lit the pipe with a vesta and gratefully revelled in the acrid blue smoke. The police sergeant drove the big motor car away as we strode along the towpath in a direction which Grimes assured us would take us to Popper's Island. We walked for perhaps a quarter of a mile before we caught sight of the huge clump of greenery in mid-river which Grimes declared to be our goal. We had passed nobody else on the path and there were few craft on the river, but the inspector assured us, 'Had this been a Wednesday or a Saturday you would have seen the Greyfriars lads everywhere. On the river, on the towpath, on the bridge. The rest of the time it's pretty quiet. There is a boat-yard just ahead where we can get a craft to cross to the island, should you decide that it is necessary.' From the way he spoke I inferred that Grimes thought that Holmes might find the mere sight of Popper's Island enough. We gazed at the surrounded strip of land with interest. It was about three hundred yards long perhaps, but very narrow, and it appeared to be flanked almost entirely by willows and rushes. But the tops of other trees could be seen above these. Birds of many different species appeared to inhabit the area. Holmes surveyed the island through hooded eyes and pronounced it a pleasing sight. 'Would that the Thames had such diverting mud banks! Tell me, Inspector, will Sir Hilton Popper object to our landing on his island. Do you think we should engage his permission?'

The burly police inspector was a practical man. He said, 'He might well object, but then a lot of red tape might be involved if I seek official sanction. I suggest we nip over and see what we can. Should Sir Hilton or his keepers challenge us we must try and bluff it out!'

Holmes applauded, 'Splendid, Inspector. You are a man after my own heart. If we proceed quietly we may not even be detected. Come, let us procure a boat.' Holmes indicated Bullen's Boat Yard with the stem of his pipe.

We had no difficulty in obtaining a punt into which the three of us climbed. It fell to my lot to pole us over to the island where we pulled into an inlet which was obviously much used in this way. Then, having secured the punt to a post, we started our exploration of Popper's Island. We pushed our way through dense undergrowth and over-hanging branches more suggestive of a Brazilian rain-forest than a sandbank on a Kentish river. It was hard going but soon we found the pool, or pond, which Holmes was seeking. Not very large, it was yet pleasant in its shade and populated as it was by the more usual waterbirds as well as some more exotic species. Majestic black swans there were, as well as a pair of flamingos. But whilst these birds were of great interest they did not divert Holmes from finding that which he was seeking. Soon he had discovered a clump of the weed which he alone among us would have recognized for what it was.

'There you see, Inspector, Watson, there it is! I venture to say that this is the only place in the county, possibly even in the country, where this weed could be found. Our quarry could have been here. I say *could*, because it is possible that others have come into contact with this clump of weed, yet who are innocent of all save entering the murdered man's shop.'

I asked, 'Could those leaves not have been trampled into the shop at a much earlier date?' Grimes shook his head, saying, 'Old Silverman kept that shop like a new pin . . . swept it twice a day sometimes.'

But suddenly all our conjectures were abruptly ended as a sharp voice of the kind that has given a lot of orders in its time, emanated from the bushes. 'Hey, you there, you fellows! Stand quite still or I'll have me keeper blow you all to kingdom come!' Grimes recognized the voice and muttered, 'Oh my lord, it's Sir Hilton.' Then the tall, erect figure of the baronet himself emerged from the undergrowth. He wore country tweeds, sported a cap, and a monocle gleamed in front of his left eye beneath a huge grey eyebrow, a close match to his military moustache. He was tanned, elderly and extremely autocratic. Following him closely was a small, shifty-looking man in riding breeches, and with a rifle held at the ready. Grimes was apologetic and diplomatic. He said, 'Sir Hilton, I should have contacted you before setting foot on your island, but when I tell you that I am conducting an urgent murder enquiry you will understand that I have had little time for niceties!'

Sir Hilton growled, 'By George, it's Grimes! I was expectin' it to be some poacher. Who are these rum-lookin' johnnies with you?' I wasn't sure that I liked being referred to as a rum-looking johnny, but said nothing. Grimes introduced us, 'Sherlock Holmes, Dr Watson, Sir Hilton Popper.'

'Sherlock Holmes eh?' Evidently Sir Hilton had heard of my friend. 'Bless my soul! Well, you are lucky, the three of you. If me dog had been here she would have ripped you to bits. Poor devil died last night . . . don't know why . . . but me man here, Forbes, found her dead last night and buried her. Dashed fine dog too, had her for years. Darn shame, what?' The baronet tugged at his moustache and was not quite dry eyed. Holmes spoke kindly to the old gentleman. 'Sir Hilton, you were fond of your dog, yet you allowed her to be out here on the island at night?' The baronet replied, 'That was her job, watchdog you know. But Forbes stays here at night in his hut, so she was not alone.'

Holmes turned to Forbes, asking, 'You found the dog dead, Mr Forbes? What was the cause of her death?' The keeper replied with bad grace, 'Dunno. She was a lyin' there dead, so I buried her.'

Grimes probably had no more idea than I did as to why Holmes was interested in the demise of the dog, but backed him up, asking Forbes, 'Where did you bury her?' Forbes jerked a thumb and said, 'Other side of the pond.' He clearly wished to drop the subject. This I could tell increased Holmes's interest. He asked Sir Hilton, 'May we see the grave?'

The baronet, a little puzzled I think, led us over to the far side of the pond, which was equally secluded from the opposite river bank. There we inspected the mound of fresh earth and Holmes dropped his bombshell. He said, 'Sir Hilton, I would like your permission to disinter your dog.'

'What?' The monocle dropped from the old man's eye. 'I say, look here, what has me poor old Jess got to do with this murder that you are investigatin', what?' Holmes replied, 'The manner in which the dog died may have some bearing on the murder, Sir Hilton.' Through long experience of association with Holmes I could tell that it was Forbes that he was observing as he spoke. The gamekeeper took on an expression of shiftiness as he appealed to the baronet. 'Look 'ere, Sir 'Ilton, what I says is this 'ere . . . it just ain't right digging up the poor animal. That just ain't right!' I felt that Sir Hilton agreed with Forbes, but after standing for a while and staring at us all in turn he said, 'Very well, if it's the right thing to do. Fetch the spade, Forbes. Hurry now, man!'

Muttering and protesting the keeper entered a nearby shed and emerged with a spade. Sir Hilton bade him dig and he set to work, although one could hardly say that he did so with a will. Although he worked slowly he could not for long put off the moment when the poor dog was revealed. It was a huge and ancient labrador of grizzled appearance. As the head appeared the baronet turned away, dabbing at his eye and muttering to the effect that he had got dust in it. The unwilling workman stood back in a surly manner as Holmes bent down and examined the beast's head. There was a wound between the eyes. Holmes said, in some surprise, 'But this poor creature has been shot! I understood that the dog had died from natural causes.'

Sir Hilton glared at Forbes and enquired, 'What is the meaning of this, man? You told me you found her dead!' Forbes stood well back and said, 'She attacked me . . . I had to shoot her!' 'Nonsense!' The old baronet was all but apoplectic in his anger.

Holmes turned to me and said, 'Watson, do you think you could remove the bullet? You are so much more adept at such things than I.' I removed the bullet from the poor creature's skull, not with the appropriate instrument but with a penknife. I handed the lead bullet to Holmes who studied it before handing it to Grimes. As he did so, he said, 'Inspector, if you compare this bullet with the one that killed Silverman I think you will find that it was fired from the same gun. Notice the groove down one side. Such imperfections are never identical from gun to gun, I can recognize the similarity having seen the bullet that you showed me but once!'

As I stood away from the grave Holmes walked back to it and bent down to further inspect the loose soil. Suddenly his long, slim fingers worked hard, and triumphantly he removed a leather pouch with a drawstring. He held it aloft. Grimes took the pouch impatiently from Holmes and hastily opened its mouth. He gazed inside, then said, 'Watches, rings, a pearl necklace! I think when they are more closely examined they will prove to be those which were the undoing of poor old Silverman. Mr Forbes, I think you have got rather a lot of explaining to do!'

But Forbes had sprung into sudden action. Flinging the spade aside he leapt over to the shed, against the side of which leant the gun. He grabbed and raised the weapon, aiming it at Inspector Grimes, saying, 'All right, copper, you can throw over that pouch or I'll blow your head off.

The rest of you stand well back, I assure you this thing is loaded!'

Grimes threw him the pouch and Holmes and I stepped back. But the old baronet stood his ground and I was terrified that he was going to try and chance his arm. Forbes rapped out more orders. 'Stand perfectly still, the lot of you. Remember I'm for the drop anyway if I'm nabbed, so I'm not going to let you raise the alarm. You blokes better all start saying your prayers. But don't pray for me, I'll be all right, you bank on it. I'll be across the Channel in Sir Hilton's motor launch before the night's out! Perhaps you didn't know that it was tied up on this side of the island, Inspector. His lordship 'ere doesn't go about in no rowing boat!'

Grimes gritted his teeth, saying, 'Forbes, don't be a fool. Hand me that gun and give yourself up!' But there was not a lot of conviction in his voice, no great belief that Forbes would do anything of the kind. After all, as he had said, he had nothing to lose. My own mind was working overtime. I realized that to shoot us all he would have to reload. That would be my chance to spring into action, assuming that I were not among the first to be shot. The flaw was that I could hardly stand and watch the others being killed before my very eyes.

Then the old baronet spoke out. 'Hand me that gun at once, Forbes! You'll have to kill me if you don't because I'm going to take it from you!' I had never seen anything so brave as this tactic of the old soldier. He knew that if Forbes shot him, the rest of us might have a chance to make a concerted effort. But as the baronet moved forward and Forbes sighted the gun a most incredible thing happened. A lithe figure, that of a schoolboy as it transpired, dropped neatly onto the gamekeeper's shoulders, as if from the sky! I realized that he had in fact dropped from a tree as I leapt forward to disarm the fallen criminal. So stunned was Forbes that he offered no resistance. Within seconds Grimes had handcuffed the man's hands behind his back. He grinned wryly as he said, 'We may not be able to carry firearms, but thank heavens for the bracelets!'

Just as soon as we could fully believe in our deliverance we turned our attention to the being who had dropped, as if delivered by providence in our moment of need. Certainly Sir Hilton Popper owed his life to this impudent-looking schoolboy who stood before us. Holmes asked, 'May I enquire your name, young sir, that I might thank you formally for your brave and timely action?' The boy, who wore a Greyfriars uniform, replied, 'My name is Herbert Vernon-Smith of the Greyfriars Remove. I've been up in the tree all along, so I sized up the jolly old situation and knew what I had to do. Couldn't very well just stay up there and see Sir Hilton shot!' I said, 'What you did took calculation and cool courage.' He laughed rather bitterly as he replied, 'Well, at Greyfriars they do call me the Bounder!' Grimes asked, 'Master Vernon-Smith, whilst I cannot thank you enough for what you have done, I must still ask you what you are doing here on Popper's Island when you should, I feel sure, be at the school?'

The Bounder laughed drily and said, 'I knew that I was about to be accused of something rather serious, but something that for once I had not done. I knew that old Quelch would accuse me and there were circumstances that would make it seem as if he was right. So last night I hooked it, and thought I'd hang out here on the island and hide in the hope that the real culprit might be found.

I told only my pal, Redwing, and I knew he wouldn't give me away. I found a suitable log and floated over, though it wasn't easy . . . I got rather damp! I thought I would sleep in the keeper's hut and managed to get in through the window. I was looking around the hut for something to eat when I found the bag with the jewels in it. However, I didn't touch it for it was no concern of mine. After sleeping a while I heard a dog bark. I climbed out of the window and hid in the bushes. To my horror I saw Forbes shoot the dog in the head, and bury it along with the pouch, which I knew to contain jewels. Then he left, and I heard the boat engine, so I climbed back into the shed and went to sleep. I hung around here this morning and when Sir Hilton and Forbes arrived I hid in the tree. I think you know the rest.' There was a touch of sarcasm in his voice.

Sir Hilton Popper, who had for some minutes stood as if turned to stone, suddenly became animated. He grasped Vernon-Smith by the hand and pumped it smartly, saying, 'Young man, that was dashed brave of you and I owe you my life. If you are in some sort of trouble at the school, remember I'm one of the governors and I will do all I can to help you!'

Vernon-Smith spoke bitterly, 'Thank you, sir, but no one will believe me, or even you. You see, I'm the Bounder of the school and that is that! I'll just have to face the sack, though heaven knows what the pater will say. I've given him enough trouble already.'

Real concern and humanity showed in Sir Hilton's face as he said, 'I say, look here Holmes, you are a detective. What if I were to pay your fee, or whatever your charge is called, could you investigate this matter? This is a splendid young chap and I feel sure that he is innocent of whatever he is accused of!'

Holmes smiled. 'Sir Hilton, Inspector, let me explain. I have already been called in over this particular affair at Greyfriars. But it is a delicate matter in that I have promised to keep it confidential.'

Grimes said, 'As I have not received any complaint from the school I need not intrude.'

Holmes nodded gratefully and then said to Vernon-Smith, 'Rest assured young sir, that I will solve the problem which worries you so there will be no need for you to absent yourself any longer from the school. If you would like me to, I will explain this to Dr Locke, and tell him of your brave action. I feel sure this would cause him to waive any punishment regarding your absence.'

Vernon-Smith said, 'Thank you, Mr Holmes, but I think not. I'll only get a whoppin' for being out of bounds. It's the other matter that might lead to a sacking. But I don't mind going back now that I know that you are around to see fair play.'

Holmes replied, 'It is unjust that you should be punished at all after the service that you have rendered us. But you are responsible enough to decide. I can only go along with your wishes and redouble my efforts.' He added, wryly, 'If only to save Mr Quelch's reputation for being just!'

The baronet tugged at Holmes's sleeve and asked quietly, 'I say, it's not a woman or anything like that, is it?' The detective chuckled and shook his head. Sir Hilton muttered, 'Well, one never knows these days, what?'

I glanced at my watch and reminded them that it was time to return to the punt.

Sir Hilton, however, would not hear of this, saying, 'Come, there is ample room for us all in the launch, passengers and prisoner alike.' So we travelled back to the towpath in style, Sir Hilton steering, and towing the punt behind us.

CHAPTER FOUR

The Bounder's Return

The sun showed distinct signs of being past its midday mark by the time we had returned the punt to the boatyard. We said our goodbyes to the formidable Sir Hilton Popper, who thanked us profusely in turn. We reached the waste ground where we knew we would find the inspector's car. I was amused to see the police sergeant's open-mouthed expression of amazement at the sight of the manacled criminal. He protested, 'Inspector, you've arrested Sir Hilton Popper's gamekeeper, Forbes!' Grimes grinned in triumph and said, 'I have arrested the murderer of Silverman the jeweller. What is more I have recovered his ill-gotten gains! It was a remark of Mr Holmes here that put me on the right track.' As they bundled the criminal into the car I mused upon how quickly the police inspector had started to take on the manner of counterparts at Scotland Yard. It could have been Lestrade talking! He asked, 'Can I drop you at the Cross Keys, gentlemen?'

We declined we had decided to accompany Vernon-Smith to Greyfriars, and as the big limousine purred on its way Forbes glared at us through the back window. His most venomous glare was directed at Holmes.

As we chatted with Vernon-Smith on our way to the school, I asked, 'Why do you think that Mr Quelch has what appears to be a down on you?'

But it was Holmes who answered. He said, 'Oh come, Watson. No form-master can entirely approve of a member of his class who breaks bounds at night, smokes cigarettes and plays nap at the Cross Keys.'

Vernon-Smith wheeled to face Holmes and with a curl of his lip said, 'Oh, I see, you have been spying on me. Well, perhaps you think you are entitled to do that, but there are certain things a decent chap does not do.'

Holmes replied, 'No, I have not spied upon you, though I am not a decent chap, I am a consulting detective . . . or rather, I was.'

The Bounder retorted, 'Some sneak has told you those things, then!'

'Why no, it was all quite obvious. To begin with, nicotine stains are almost impossible to remove from the fingers, however hard one scrubs. As for the illicit card games at the Cross Keys, why, Watson and I are staying at that dubious hostelry. Only last night I saw a junior boy from Greyfriars taking part in a game of nap. I overheard him ask whether old Smithy had been in. As for breaking bounds, I hardly imagine the rules allow junior boys to be out of gates at ten at night.' Then Holmes chuckled and added, 'Apart from all this your form-master filled me in on your background!'

'I see . . .' The Bounder coloured slightly. 'I guess I owe

you an apology, Mr Holmes.' But my friend was dismissive of this necessity, saying, 'Think nothing of it, my dear chap. We have more important worries, you and I!'

Of course, Herbert Vernon-Smith's troubles did indeed begin the very moment we entered the school gates. Gosling, the porter, was the first to spot him, saying, 'There you are, you young rip. The 'ole school 'as been lookin' for yer! What I says is this 'ere. You've got to go straight to Mr Quelch's study and be quick abaht it!' A crowd of the junior boys were punting a football about in the quad. They stopped abruptly as they saw Vernon-Smith.

'Gosh, it's Smithy . . . the jolly old wanderer returns!'

'The returnfulness is terrific!'

Soon Smithy was surrounded by his class mates, most of them delighted that he was safe, and much concerned for his future well-being. They vied with each other to give advice and good-natured greetings. His friend and study mate, Redwing, said, 'Smithy, old man, Quelch is really waxy, you know. Better go to his study and get it over with.'

The Bounder replied, 'Just what I'm going to do, Reddy. Don't worry, I'll see you in the study later.'

As we neared the entrance to the school building we encountered the fat junior, Bunter, leaning against a wall and demolishing a packet of toffee. He grinned all over his fat, sticky face as he advised, 'I say, Smithy, if you are going to see Quelch I should stuff a few exercise books down your bags! He, he, he!' Bunter emitted a fat chuckle in anticipation of the Bounder's fate. Vernon-Smith said, 'Mr Holmes, Doctor, will you excuse me whilst I kick that fat fool?' We gladly nodded our assent and the Bounder pursued the now fearful fat owl of the Remove who put on quite a spurt of speed for one so portly. Thud! A well-directed boot delivered a swift kick upon the tightest trousers in the whole county of Kent. 'Yarooh . . . beast . . . cad . . . rotter . . . yah!' Bunter scuttled away and Vernon-Smith rejoined us.

The corridor known as Masters' Studies was soon reached, and by the time we stood outside the door bearing Mr Quelch's name the Bounder had regained his cool manner. I knocked upon the door. 'Enter!' The Remove master's voice was acidic enough for Vernon-Smith to murmur, 'Henry's waxy!'

As Mr Quelch rose from the chair behind his desk the glimmer of a smile, intended for Holmes and myself, disappeared, to be replaced by an angry frown as his eyes lit upon Herbert Vernon-Smith, the Bounder of the Greyfriars Remove.

'So, Vernon-Smith, you have returned.' Quelch could scarcely temper the fury in his voice as he turned his attention to us. 'Mr Holmes, Dr Watson, I must postpone the pleasure of your company for a short while in order that I might deal with an urgent school matter.' His hand closed around the handle of his cane which he obviously intended to wield. This intention, however, was prevented, or at the very least postponed, by Holmes's words.

'Mr Quelch, what I have come here to say has connection with the comings and goings of this young rascal. Indeed, I would like to speak on his behalf if I may.'

Quelch breathed long and hard, but the grasp upon the handle of his cane relaxed, as indeed did his manner though only very slightly. He said, 'Mr Holmes, as I am indebted to you for your efforts on my behalf concerning a certain matter so I can scarcely refuse your request. Pray be seated, gentlemen. Vernon-Smith, you may stand near the book-case.'

For the five minutes that followed, Holmes gave Quelch a résumé of the day's events and our adventures. The school-master's jaw began to slacken and his eyes grew rounder. My friend finished his oration by saying, 'So, Sir Hilton Popper and possibly Watson and I owe our lives to the quick thinking and swift reaction, aye and real heroic courage, of this young gentleman. With all of this in mind I would ask you not to punish him for breaking bounds and absenting himself from school. Little reward enough for such heroism. As for the other matter, Vernon-Smith has not as yet been accused, let alone found guilty. I have questioned him regarding the disappearance of the manuscript. He assures me that he knows nothing of this matter. I am inclined to believe him, although of course you may not. However, in view of the fact that my investigations are far from completed, I suggest that you postpone further questioning or accusation until such time as they are.'

Holmes's oratory was strong, and although Quelch was obviously far from convinced of the Bounder's innocence he could scarcely refuse the request. He was thoughtful for some moments and then, turning his head towards the Bounder, said, 'Vernon-Smith, without the intervention of Mr Holmes I would have caned you severely for ab-senting yourself from Greyfriars. Whatever the circumstances, I would have been justified in so doing. I would like to think that some suspicion that I may hold concerning your involvement in another matter would not have affected the severity of such just punishment. However, I am led to believe that you have performed a very brave action and for this I commend you. Regarding that certain other matter, I will reserve any further action, opinion or judgement until Mr Holmes has completed certain enquiries. Now you may go and rejoin your school fellows.'

'Yes, sir, thank you, sir.' The Bounder nodded politely to Holmes and myself as he left the room.

The Remove master pursed his lips and placed the tips of his fingers together and said, 'I hope, Mr Holmes, that you feel that I have behaved justly. I have always prided myself on being just . . . Stern . . . but just. However, but for your intervention I might have behaved unjustly, and so I thank you.'

We bade Mr Quelch good night and emerged from his study to find a changed atmosphere in the school. The subject of the theft and the identity of the man investigating it had passed from rumour to established knowledge during less than an hour. There were not many boys in the vicinity of the masters' studies, but plenty of them in the corridor which housed the juniors' studies and their common-room, or the rag as it was known. We had only to stand for a moment or two outside the rag to hear a babble of relevant conversation.

'I say, you fellows, did you see the jolly old sleuth?'

'We did, old fat man. What about him?'

'Oh nothing, except that his friend insisted on standing me a feed at the tuck shop!'

'Rot!'

'Gammon!'

'Fact, and I never told him that I had been disappointed about a postal order . . .'

'Ha, ha, ha!'

'Say, who do you guys think snaffled the old guy's manuscript?'

'Blessed if I know, Fishy. Ask Toddy, he's the jolly old lawyer, or rather his pater is!'

'Well, Toddy, what's the score?'

'I'm sure Smithy is innocent . . . not his game . . . I submit. How about you, Fishy, you buy and sell almost anything. Have you found a buyer for *The History of Greyfriars?*'

'Ha, ha, ha!'

We smiled, not putting too much store in schoolboy accusations.

On the towpath, Holmes, happy to have prevented an injustice, returned to the matter of Quelch and his missing manuscript. Several hundred closely written pages upon the school history would not appear to be a glittering prize for theft or of a great deal of use to anyone but Henry Samuel Quelch. 'It can only be some kind of an act of revenge or a schoolboy prank. No burglar or sneak thief would take it, neatly labelled so that its subject and author could not be in doubt.' He added, 'Did you feel, Watson, that at our first interview there was something in Mr Quelch's manner that was less than frank?' I replied, 'He did appear a little guarded, but I put it down to anxiety at the time.'

When we finally got back to the Cross Keys the evening was well advanced and we dined upon a tolerable cold mutton joint washed down with some all but undrinkable house wine. However, the cheese was passable. We spent the rest of the evening nursing our tankards in the snug, with Holmes in a reverie. His brown study was interrupted not by myself but by voices from an ante-room. The owners of these voices were hidden from our view by a heavy curtain.

'It's fifteen quid you owes me altogether, Master Skinner!'

'But if you let me play another hand I feel sure that I can put things right!'

'No more credit, and I'm afraid I shall 'ave to come up to the school and see your 'eadmaster about it if you don't pay up soon!'

'But Mr Banks, you know that would mean the sack for me!'

'Can't 'elp that, I've got to keep everything straight for my haccountant. Next Thursday night or I really will come up there. You'd better cut 'orf now as you've got no credit!'

The two voices, the one beery and knowing, the other youthful and fearful, told their own story. The owner of the youthful voice emerged through the curtain, his cap and tweed jacket doing little to disguise his public-school status. I said to Holmes, 'Sad, especially as he is a Greyfriars lad!'

'Very sad, Watson, but it is not a matter that we can poke an oar into.'

That night, before we turned in, I asked Holmes if it were too early to ask him where he thought that Quelch's manuscript might be and who could have purloined it. He replied, 'In a word, Watson, yes! By which I mean that it is too early as yet. As for suspects, as I believe the writers of detective stories now express it. (You have something to answer for, my dear fellow, for starting a trend which I cannot call a literary one!) Well, there are several quite promising candidates. Of course, we cannot as yet entirely eliminate Vernon-Smith despite our feelings in his favour.

He has many good qualities but is, after all, the Bounder and according to his reputation not renowned for truthfulness.'

I asked, 'How about Fish, the American boy?'

'I have considered him, Watson, but only because he appears to have a business sense far beyond his years.'

'And Peter Todd? He also seems canny.'

'Yes, but in a different way and far too well aware of the punishment that the law would bring upon the culprit!'

'Bunter then?'

Holmes threw back his head and laughed, 'Come Watson, he is greedy, untruthful and crafty in a foolish sort of way. But he has not the courage of a rabbit!'

'How about the staff?'

'You have met them. Can you spot a criminal in their midst?'

'How about the language master, Carpentier? He is French!'

Holmes chuckled, 'Oh, my dear Watson, I do wish you would try to put Waterloo out of your mind!'

I retired early, leaving Holmes still sitting in the snug, and I was happy to notice that he had his favourite clay and a pouch full of the Scottish Mixture that had so often in the past seemed to be the prelude to a problem solved.

CHAPTER FIVE

The Search Begins

We were out and about at an unusually early hour on the following morning, Holmes deciding that we would give breakfast a miss. This did not please me but I made no protest. He seemed in need of a good brisk country walk and, without seeming knowledge of his goal or direction, began to cross a small stone bridge. At the other end of it I noticed a youthful figure in a Greyfriars uniform, holding some sort of despatch case. I remarked to Holmes that it was too early for one of the schoolboys to be out and about. The boy, tall for a junior, with long, lank hair and a prominent nose, raised his cap to us as we arrived at the spot upon which he stood. He said, politely, 'Good morning, gentlemen.'

To my surprise Holmes replied, 'Good morning, Master Todd.' Curiously, the schoolboy lawyer had figured in our conversations, but I for one had not set eyes upon him that I could remember.

The boy started a little, 'I didn't think we had met.'

Holmes said, 'Indeed we have not, but last evening upon passing the junior common room we could not help but hear the name Todd being spoken, coupled with the knowledge that the owner of that name was the son of a solicitor.'

'But you did not see me.'

'No, but I recognize the style of your despatch case as being one favoured by the legal profession. It is an elderly case and has received more wear than you could have given it, in even several years of hard use. I therefore deduce that it has been passed on to you by its original owner. The most likely happening would be for a solicitor to have passed the case on to his son to end its days as a school bag. Now that I am able to inspect it more closely I can see that my deduction was correct, for the bag bears the initials T T and T. These I imagine are those of Todd, Todd and Todd, a law firm well known to me by reputation.'

Master Todd, far from being slack-jawed with astonishment, said, 'Brilliantly deduced Mr Holmes, and I assume that your companion is Dr Watson. I knew you were in the vicinity, and your conversation has hardly been that of a plumber or dairy farmer!'

The boy excused himself upon the grounds of an appointment and raising his cap again he smartly took himself off in the direction of a clump of woodland. As soon as he was out of earshot I said, 'Holmes, do you not think it singular for a Remove boy to be keeping an appointment at a time when he might be expected to be at breakfast with his form-mates?'

Holmes answered, 'I do, especially as he is carrying a despatch case easily large enough to hold a four-hundred-page manuscript!'

Holmes agreed with me when I said that we should not jump to any conclusions, saying, 'I think I must stalk our young friend to ascertain the nature of his appointment. Stay here, my dear fellow, I will do it more easily alone. I may be gone for some time; on the other hand, I might be back within a matter of a few minutes.'

He took himself off in the direction that young Todd, now hidden from our view by the trees, had taken. I sat upon the stone edge of the bridge parapet and started a pipe full of shag. I was not offended by Holmes's wish to do his stalking alone for I knew that one person can conceal himself more easily than can two. He was gone for about ten minutes, judging from the way my tobacco had behaved. I could see that he was finding it difficult to keep a straight face. He sat down beside me and began to charge his own pipe as he said, 'Oh Watson, how wrong we were! Far from containing Quelch's manuscript, that case was stuffed with law books. You will not believe this, Watson, but young Todd, in return for five shillings, was giving Banks the bookmaker some advice on the legality or otherwise of certain betting practices!'

I whistled softly, 'How like such an unsavoury character to try to get his legal advice on the cheap!'

Holmes said, 'I almost laughed aloud, but could not lest I betrayed my hiding place in a thicket!'

At a sensible hour we made our way to Greyfriars to call upon Dr Locke. His greetings to us, although kindly and sincere, held the slightest whisper of impatience. Although he did not say he was a very busy man, I detected his mood. After all, Dr Locke had himself appealed to me to use my influence with Holmes. Of course Holmes felt this too but contented himself with saying, 'Dr Locke, we will not long presume upon your time, but I know that the recovery of Mr Quelch's manuscript is possibly of more concern to yourself than it is to us.' He could always turn a phrase which would put a person in his place. He was a master of this as he was of so much else.

The headmaster realized that he had bordered upon being most unjustly brusque. He said, 'My dear Mr Holmes, forgive me. I am entirely at your disposal.'

Holmes replied, 'May I suggest that in order to make progress as quickly as we might all desire, the following two steps might be taken? First, I think it would be a good idea to have a search made of all the junior studies, if only to allay suspicions in certain directions. Second, I have drafted a message that I would like posted upon the school notice-board.'

Dr Locke touched the electric bell-push on his desk as he said, 'I will act immediately upon your first suggestion.' He took a gold hunter from his waistcoat pocket, studied it, and then replaced it. 'There is time for the search to be carried out during second lesson. But regarding the notice, I would of course have to approve it before giving permission for its display.'

'Of course, my dear Dr Locke. I have it here.' Holmes took the paper upon which he had neatly written the notice and handed it to the headmaster. But the good doctor's perusal of it was interrupted by a tap on the door of his study.

'Enter!'

A fine-looking youth of athletic build and some seventeen years respectfully entered the room. He asked, 'You sent for me, Headmaster?'

'Ah yes, Wingate. You are the prefect on duty and I need

you.' Dr Locke turned to Holmes and asked, 'I take it, sir, that you have no objection to Wingate being taken into our confidence. He is the head boy of the school and enjoys my trust.'

We both nodded to Wingate, and Holmes said, 'I feel sure that young Wingate could be of great help to us.' Dr Locke and Sherlock Holmes between them explained the matter of the investigation to the sixth-form prefect. Wingate whistled softly, then cleared his throat and said, 'I beg your pardon, Headmaster, but . . . but jolly old Quelch's manuscript is as much part of this school as the clock tower or Mrs Mimble's tuck shop! I had heard rumours but discounted them.' Dr Locke nodded in approval, saying, 'Quite so, but unfortunately in this case rumour proves to be founded upon fact. Mr Holmes wishes you to assist him in his investigations by searching the junior studies whilst the boys are at second lesson.'

Holmes added, 'You see, Wingate, I don't particularly expect you to find the missing manuscript . . . by the way, it is foolscap, several hundred sheets, hand-written and tied with string . . . but look out for anything unusual, anything that you might not expect to find in a schoolboy's study. Rather it should be you than me because even if you are seen in one of the studies it will not be considered unusual.'

'Rather not, Mr Holmes. I have had to search studies many times before. Missing tuck hampers, that sort of thing. On the last occasion crumbs from a fruit cake and some peach stones found in Bunter's study proved to be the clues that I needed!'

I laughed, and Holmes said, 'Elementary, eh, my dear Wingate?'

After Wingate had departed to set about his detective work, Dr Locke returned to his perusal of Holmes's notice. He read it aloud in a clear voice, touched but lightly with the quaver that comes with age . . .

LOST OR STOLEN! A MANUSCRIPT, THE PROPERTY OF H S QUELCH MA. FOUR HUNDRED FOOLSCAP SHEETS, THE TOP SHEET CLEARLY MARKED 'THE HISTORY OF GREYFRIARS'. THE WHOLE BOUND WITH GREEN STRING AND SEALED WITH RED WAX. MR QUELCH'S STUDY WILL REMAIN UN- LOCKED THROUGHOUT THIS EVENING. SHOULD THE MANUSCRIPT REAPPEAR UPON HIS DESK NO FURTHER ACTION WILL BE TAKEN.

When he had finished reading the notice Dr Locke said, 'A rather benevolent attitude to take, I feel. I would myself prescribe a flogging or even expulsion for the culprit. How- ever, I do appreciate Mr Quelch's anxiety to regain his manuscript. I will be guided entirely by you, my dear Holmes. You have a free hand!' The headmaster rose to his feet, indicating that the interview was at an end.

The result of Wingate's search proved disappointing, unearthing only the remains of a pie, which had been missed from the school kitchen by Mrs Kebble, the house- keeper, and a fives bat neatly marked with the owner's name, Peter Todd. The latter was discovered in a study occupied by Hurree Jamset Ram Singh. However, Master Todd later dismissed the matter by saying, 'I lent it to Inky to pulverize Bunter with!' As for the fat owl of the Remove himself, he denied all knowledge of the pie but managed to condemn himself with his own stupidity, saying, 'I never got up in the middle of the night and nabbed that pie . . . such a thing would never occur to me! You can ask Fishy if you like because I gave him a slice . . . not that I had the pie anyway!' Needless to say, Mr Quelch's cane descended six times upon the largest seat at Greyfriars School, or possibly even in the entire county of Kent, or maybe in the whole of England.

Whack!

'Yarooh!'

Whack!

'Wroogh, grough!'

Whack!

'Ooh stoppit . . . yarooh!'

Whack, whack, whack!

'Oh crikey, help, yarooh!'

The fat junior crawled rather than walked out of Quelch's study and dragged himself along the corridor, where Holmes and I were standing. Before creeping away he glared at Holmes through his big spectacles and muttered 'Beast . . . yah!' I said, 'You must forgive him, Holmes. He is obviously the victim of a glandular condition which has sharpened his appetite at the expense of his wits!'

We absented ourselves from the school during the earlier part of the evening to return only after the juniors had been confined to their dorms. Then we tapped upon Mr Quelch's study door, and although he bade us enter he did not rise and greet us with his usual polite acidity as we did so. One could almost describe him as being slumped across his desk. Bitterly he said, 'Mr Holmes, your ploy has produced a result, though not I fear the one for which we had hoped.' He passed us a portion torn from a sheet of foolscap bearing the word 'The History of . . .' the words written in Quelch's own copperplate. He continued, 'As you will see, it is torn from the title sheet of my manuscript. I returned a short while ago to find it lying on my desk alongside a scrap of paper with a message pencilled upon it.' He passed a second fragment to Holmes.

The paper was pink in colour and rough of quality. Between the lines of printed matter the pencilled message was there:

IF YOU WANT THE REST OF YOUR RUBBISH BACK, LEAVE FIFTEEN POUNDS IN AN ENVELOPE ON THE CLOISTERS SUNDIAL TOMORROW NIGHT AT TEN. TELL NO ONE OF THIS AND THE MANU-SCRIPT WILL BE RETURNED UNHARMED.

Holmes said, 'I am grateful to find that I have your complete confidence Mr Quelch, for had I not you might have been tempted to have kept this message to yourself, complied with its instructions and possibly even regained your manuscript for a fairly modest sum. Who can say that this is not what you should do? Although I think you have that sense of right and justice that would prevent you from taking the easy way out.'

Quelch all but snapped at Holmes, 'Of course I will not give in to blackmail, sir, and although you may consider fifteen pounds to be a trifling sum, I, sir, do not!'

I tried to reduce the tension of the situation by enquiring of Holmes, 'Can you deduce anything from the pencilled message?' He shrugged, 'Not a great deal, Watson, except that the paper is torn from a sporting news sheet, its colour tells me that. It is from an early edition, which I can tell from the amount of space between the paragraphs of print. The last edition, for example, would leave hardly any space at all. The message has been written with an HB pencil and the paper was rested upon a ser-rated surface.'

Quelch asked, impatiently, 'D'ye think it might have been written by a junior boy of this school?'

Holmes could not be sure. 'It is possible. It has been neatly written and the spelling is correct, but I imagine that this would not place it beyond the range of a number of boys in your class.'

Quelch replied, 'Yes, but it would eliminate some of them . . . Bunter for example . . .'

The detective asked, 'Who, Mr Quelch, in your opinion of all your boys would be the most likely to own a racing journal?'

The school-master's reply was swift, perhaps a trifle too swift. 'Vernon-Smith! I have had to punish him on a number of occasions for gambling and once he even had the temerity to attend the Wapshot races!'

But Holmes and I both felt that Mr Quelch was jumping too quickly upon the possibility of the Bounder of the Remove being the writer of the note. Holmes in fact gently expressed the thought by suggesting, 'Surely among the thirty or so boys in your class there are others capable of having the nerve to own a racing paper?'

Reluctantly, Quelch considered and said, 'Why yes, there are other black sheep in my fold . . . Stott . . . Snoop . . . Skinner, for example. But I think they are just weak and misguided, whereas Vernon-Smith . . .'

I could not help but interject, 'Oh come, sir, give a dog a bad name, what?'

The Remove master nodded and said, 'I take your point, Doctor, but Mr Holmes, how then should I proceed in this matter?'

Holmes's reply surprised me as well as Quelch. He said, 'If you value your manuscript do absolutely nothing!'

It was the school-master's turn to surprise me when he replied, 'The matter is now desperately important, because my publisher requires to see this first instalment. I have to go to London tomorrow afternoon to see him!'

Holmes then dropped his bombshell by saying, 'Don't worry, Mr Quelch. I have every confidence that I may be able to resolve the matter before then.'

As Quelch shook our hands some of his composure had returned.

Once we were clear of the immediate vicinity of the school Holmes voiced that which was in my own mind. 'Watson, where is the sudden urgency for a manuscript, or rather the first portion of it, that has taken its author ten years to write and which at that rate he may not even live to complete?'

I ventured, 'Could the manuscript be a figment of Quelch's imagination?'

'You mean is he quite mad, with delusions of literary grandeur? I think not, Watson, for many persons at the school can bear witness to his constant preoccupation with his *History* over many years. No, it is just this sudden urgency that worries me. I would dearly love to follow him to London and see if he really does visit a publisher! However, first things first and there is work to be done locally.'

I hardly needed to volunteer for I knew that Holmes had me in mind to shadow Mr Quelch. But I went through the motions, saying, 'I would be glad to trail him for you whilst you attend to these urgent matters.' Holmes said, 'My dear fellow, I knew I could rely on you!'

That night in the bar of the Cross Keys, the bookmaker,

Banks, along with a few of his cronies, attempted to draw us into a card game. I was hardly surprised when Holmes declined the offer for both of us, but was amazed to see him pick up the cards, extract several of them from the pack and suggest a wager of a different kind. 'Gentlemen, I have a better suggestion. I will give you a chance to pick out the queen . . . "Find the Lady", I believe the pastime is called.'

He displayed a queen and two pip cards, starting to manipulate them in such a fashion that, flat on the table with their backs showing, it was indeed difficult to keep track of the queen. There was much grinning, nudging and knowing laughter from the group of bar-room layabouts and racing men who knew this particular scam. When asked to put money on the card of their choice, Banks voiced their general feeling, 'Garn, think we wuz born yesterday?'

At this point I observed one of Banks's cronies nudge his friend and point to the cards. I followed their gaze and noticed that which Holmes had evidently not; there was a slight bend on one of the corners of the queen, making it easy enough to follow its progress. The fellow who had noticed it said, 'Orl right, guv, I'm a sportsman, I'll 'ave a bob on this one!' He dropped a shilling onto the back of the card which obviously had to be the queen. Holmes turned the cards over and of course the queen proved to be the card chosen by the loafer. Holmes threw down a shilling to match that of his punter. Banks had evidently noticed the bent corner too and was interested now. As Holmes moved the cards around again Banks took a sovereign from his pocket, and when the long slim fingers had ceased to move the cards he dropped the sovereign onto the back of the card with the bent corner which I knew had to be the

queen. Holmes turned the cards over and of course was forced to throw down a sovereign of his own. I was amazed that Holmes, such a keen observer, had not noticed the bend in the card and tried to whisper to him. However, I was pushed out of the way by a crowd of loafers, anxious for easy money.

But the burly Banks, dragging the back of his grubby hand across his unshaven chin, ordered his cronies back, saying to Holmes, 'Orl right, it's just you and me and we'll make it a proper bet. Ow abaht ten pun this time?' To my horror I heard Holmes ask him, 'Why not make it twenty?' Banks licked his lips greedily and said, 'Twenty pun it is then!'

No money was placed upon the table this time, but after Holmes had performed his lightning gyrations a stubby finger was pressed hard down upon the back of the card with the slightly bent corner. The bookie swept the other cards to the floor lest there should be any misunderstanding. As Banks held his card down with undue pressure Holmes asked, 'Are you quite sure that you have the card you chose . . . there is still time for us to start all over again.' Banks said, 'No chance, smart boy. I'm stickin' with this one, and you'd better pay up. Remember, I've got a bar full of witnesses!' There was a buzz of assenting voices.

Triumphantly, Banks picked the card up off the table and showed its face to his cronies without even looking at it himself, such was his self-confidence. He said, 'I'll 'ave that twenty now, mister, or you'll wish you'd never been born!'

Holmes drawled, 'On the contrary, Banks, I'll have *your* twenty pounds, for I'm sure that you are not going to be a bad loser.'

Disbelief, panic, sheer rage followed each other like a passing parade of expressions on Banks's face as he looked at the face of the card he held . . . the six of hearts, with a slightly bent corner. He shouted, 'You've tricked me you ol' bag of bones . . . you've cheated me you swindlin' shyster . . . you can whistle for the twenty pun!'

Holmes's eyes widened as he said, 'That is just where you are wrong. These gentlemen are witnesses to the fair play that occurred.' The landlord, who had seen it all, spoke up. 'Joey, pay hup or never come 'ere again. You wuz twisted fair!'

Banks, possibly because he did not wish to lose his place of business, flung twenty pounds upon the table with the worst of grace, growling at Holmes, 'Mebbe I'll meet you some dark night when there h'aint't nobody abaht.' Holmes laughed and to my mounting horror said, 'Come, sir, there is no time like the present. Why do we two not step outside and settle our differences?' He held up a hand to restrain me as I attempted to join him once I realized that he was serious about fighting the bully. He said, 'Stay here, Watson, I will rejoin you shortly.' Banks muttered, 'I don't think!' as they both left the bar through its entrance door.

It was five minutes later that Holmes rejoined me. His knuckles were raw and there was a superficial cut on his lip. As he struggled just a little gingerly into his jacket he said, too loudly for it to be intended for my ears alone, 'Watson, Mr Banks is not feeling well and has decided to return to his home.' Then in more confidential tones he said to me, 'I failed to inform him that I was once the finest boxer for my weight in the whole of England. I may be somewhat elderly but my weight has not altered. The same cannot be said for Mr Banks, who is somewhat out of condition.'

I was a little worried that Banks might make some unfair complaint to the police, but Holmes did not seem to think so. 'Come, Watson, he is in no position to do that. I feel sure that his solicitor, Master Todd, would advise him against it!'

When I asked, concerning the mystery of the three-card trick, Holmes would only say, 'Watson, more than one card can have a bent corner!'

CHAPTER SIX

Mr Quelch in 'The Street of Broken Dreams'

'Come Watson, the game is afoot for you, if not for me. Pass the mustard, there's a good fellow.'

We were taking breakfast at the Cross Keys and Holmes and I were making our plans for the day. As I passed the condiment I ventured to ask, 'Do you feel that it is quite ethical for me to shadow Mr Quelch? After all, were you still in practice he would be your client!'

My friend astounded me with the flippant answer, 'But as I am not in practice any more, Watson, we can do whatever we like!' I was so surprised that I dropped some mashed potato on my cravat. As Holmes helped me to clean it off he said, 'Quelch has been less than frank with us, so he must expect my methods to be less than orthodox.

A detective might not as a rule play on both sides of the chessboard, unless he feels, as I do now, that some sort of injustice hovers.'

Thinking that I understood, I said, 'You are thinking of Vernon-Smith?'

He nodded, 'I am indeed thinking of the Bounder.'

I could think of no further reason why I should not shadow Quelch, so I asked, 'I wonder which train he will take?' But Holmes had thought of that. 'My dear fellow, there is only one train that he can take, the two-fifteen from Courtfield Junction to Charing Cross. His tutorial duties will prevent him from catching the ten-forty or midday trains. The next one is at four of the clock, so I rest my case!'

I asked, 'Shall I go in disguise?'

I was afraid for a moment that Holmes would have an hysterical fit. When he had managed to stop laughing, he said, 'Oh, forgive me, Watson old fellow, but the thought of you with a walrus moustache glued over your military appendage and wearing a suit of bookmaker's check is too bizarre to contemplate. No, I suggest that you keep well in the background and I feel sure that he will be too preoccupied to notice you.'

At about one-thirty I walked to Courtfield Junction, but after having purchased a ticket to Charing Cross I was careful not to stroll out onto the platform. For I had already espied Mr Quelch, wearing a dark overcoat and what is I believe known as a Homburg hat and carrying a bag. I watched him through a gap in the hedge, waiting for the train to actually enter the station before emerging onto the platform, in time to see the back of the school-master as he entered a carriage. I chose another, two or three down the train.

The journey was uneventful with the green fields and oast-houses of Kent giving way first to the small towns of Surrey and finally to the outskirts of the largest and greatest city in the world. Honest cockney voices in my carriage rejoiced at regaining their native turf. 'Here we are, here's the ol' Smoke!' I was the last to leave the carriage, just in time to see the angular figure of Mr Quelch as he gave his ticket to the collector. I wondered if he would take an omnibus to wherever he was bound, or perhaps one of the new taxi-cabs which had all but replaced the hansoms on the rank. He chose a taxi and I managed to hire the one immediately behind it, though not lucky enough to hear his instructions to his driver. I was forced to tell my driver, 'Just follow that cab!' He didn't question my instruction, merely muttering, 'Thinks 'e's Sherlock 'Olmes!'

Quelch's cab slowed, almost to a stop, when we had crossed the Aldwych, transforming the sedate Strand into that untidy collection of buildings that form Fleet Street. My own vehicle eventually stopped a few yards behind the spot where Quelch's taxi had arrived. Keeping a sharp eye on my quarry. I paid the driver, giving him an extra sixpence for his trouble. With typical cockney joviality he enquired of me, 'Can you recommend any good investments, Sherlock?' I did not trouble to inform him that but for me he would be as ignorant of the exploits of my friend as he was of the rules of good manners.

Mr Quelch glanced furtively around him and then crossed the street, entering a public house which I admit took me rather by surprise. I followed with difficulty, weaving my way less adroitly than he through the Fleet Street traffic. In that rather narrow thoroughfare the introduction of the internal combustion engine has added to the number of vehicles. The horse-drawn drays are still there, acting as a slow-down for the taxis and motorized omnibuses. Discreetly I followed Quelch into the saloon bar in time to see him take his grapefruit juice to a small table in the corner. As I ordered a half-pint of ale I stood at the bar with my back towards my quarry, yet able to observe his every movement in a decorative mirror.

After about five minutes Quelch arose from his seat and picked up his carpet bag. I prepared to shadow him again until I realized that he was not leaving the establishment. Instead he made for a door marked Gentlemen. Perhaps three minutes later a person other than Quelch emerged through that same door. A tall, angular man, but wearing a beret and a green corduroy jacket, his shirt open at the neck with a paisley scarf worn beneath it. Not a gentleman at all, yet . . . he was carrying Quelch's carpet bag!

Several possibilities played through my mind . . . that Quelch had delivered up his bag to someone who had waited to collect it in a public house convenience . . . that Quelch had been robbed by someone, perhaps this person, who had lain in wait for the opportunity. Or that this artistic-looking fellow simply owned an identical carpet bag. Then the truth dawned; this colourful bohemian *was* Quelch! He had been carrying a change of clothing in the carpet bag right from the start and had changed vestments in the gentlemen's toilet!

Henry Samuel Quelch did not merely look different in his artistic attire, he was quite unrecognizable. He seemed less angular and ten years younger. But not at all the sort of person to whom one would trust the education of the sons of gentlemen. It was the complete transformation.

All but open-mouthed with astonishment I practically lost my quarry, almost letting him slip away. But I brought myself to the stage where I could accept what had happened to the extent that I left the hostelry and shadowed the transformed Quelch as he strode manfully in the direction of Ludgate Hill. The only two things left about the old Quelch were a walking stick and the carpet bag.

He stopped outside an office building which, after a short pause, he entered. I did not follow him inside but waited for him to emerge, lurking in a shop doorway opposite. It was a full fifteen minutes before Quelch reappeared. I had studied the name-plate on the lintel which proclaimed the Amalgamated Press. I wondered what concerned a school-master in such an office . . . *The History of Greyfriars?* But if so, why the disguise? I decided to take a chance on Quelch's next move, thinking that he might return to the same public house to restore his normal persona. This would take him a little time, perhaps long enough to allow me to make a few enquiries. I therefore allowed him to walk swiftly in the direction of the Aldwych, myself mounting the stairs which would lead me to the offices of the Amalgamated Press.

I tapped upon a glass door and was bade 'Enter!' Inside, a rather prim-looking stenographer looked at me. 'Yes?' Her manner was hardly warm. I said, hastily inventing a new character for myself, 'My name is Falmouth, I'm a friend of Mr Quelch . . .' I waited for some friendly reaction, but came there none. I shuffled uncomfortably and at last she spoke, 'Oh yes, and who is Mr Quelch?' I was rather taken aback but swiftly realized that Quelch must have changed his name along with his attire. I recovered enough to say, 'But he was here. He left about two or three minutes ago!' She said, 'Oh, you must mean Mr Hamilton!'

At this point a door marked Editor opened and a stout man in shirt-sleeves, a cigar between his lips, emerged. He dropped some papers upon the girl's desk, then looked at me enquiringly and asked, 'Did you want to see me?' I stumbled, 'I was about to ask your secretary if Mr Quelch had left his cane here, but she tells me that only a Mr Hamilton has been here during the past few minutes.'

The editor, a jovial sort obviously, chuckled as he said, 'Oh no, that's not so! Mr Hamilton has certainly been here, but then so have Mr Clifford, Mr Richards, Mr Redway, Mr Conquest and one or two others, all within the last few minutes!' At this the miserable secretary actually started to laugh as well. In fact, they both laughed a lot at what had evidently been a joke even if its point had been completely lost on me. I stole away silently, leaving the editor and his staff to their hysterics. I remember thinking that publishers were a rum lot!

I picked up Quelch's trail again in the Strand. There he was, back in his regular attire and personality. He had evidently decided to walk the short distance to Charing Cross. I had always thought of him as a careful man, and doubtless only an imminent appointment had caused him earlier to engage a cab. From a distance I watched him climb into a Courtfield-bound train, deciding that I had risked detection enough for one day to take the same train myself. As far as I was concerned my task was over and there would have been little point in my watching Quelch during his journey back to Greyfriars. There was, I discovered, another Courtfield train at six-fifteen, which left me with a considerable wait. I retired to the station tea-room to ponder upon the strange events of the afternoon. First there was the amazing matter of Henry Samuel Quelch and his dual personality. In Stevenson's famous story a certain Dr Jekyll was able to transform himself from a respectable scientist to an evil lecher. Of course, I had no reason to believe that Quelch had taken some strange drug or potion in the men's convenience to transform himself. Moreover, his change from an academic to one of artistic appearance seemed to suggest no evil. But what business had he transacted with the Amalgamated Press under the name of Hamilton, possibly in collaboration with a Mr Richards, a Mr Redway and a Mr Clifford, among others? Why had the mention of these names created hysterical laughter in an editor and his secretary? It was a three-coffee-cup problem, but even the consumption of so much caffeine produced no answers in my mind to any of these riddles. I would simply, I decided, need to transmit my strange information to Sherlock Holmes.

Before entraining I decided to purchase some reading matter at the station bookstall. The *Strand* and *Pearson's* I had purchased before an inspiration made me enquire, 'Do you sell any publications issued by the Amalgamated Press?' 'Yes, sir, and very popular they are too!' The young man handed me two juvenile publications, *The Magnet* and *The Gem*. 'No doubt for your young nephews, eh Colonel?' The insolent fellow even tapped his nose as if these seemingly respectable schoolboy periodicals had been taken from beneath the counter. I said, 'Certainly not, I intend to peruse them myself on the train, and you have endowed me with the wrong military rank!'

I could find no first-class accommodation on the Courtfield train, which was ultimately bound for Folkestone, and had the misfortune to share a compartment with a family of Londoners en route for the sea. I had to endure all their wretched whining concerning the consumption of various eatables and drinkables from a wicker basket. They were going to the coast for a whole week, these pasty-faced cockneys, a mother, father, two boys of ten and eleven and an elderly lady addressed by them all as Aunty. It was 'Alfie, eat your sandwich and be quiet' and 'Johnny, don't pester poor Aunty' and 'Father will take 'is belt to yer', all the way to Courtfield Junction.

''Ere, guv'nor . . .' Alfie's eagle eye had spotted that I was glancing through *The Gem*. 'What's ole Baggy Trimble up to this week?' The mother's weary voice snapped, 'Don't bother the gentleman . . . He wants to read 'is comics in peace!' Alfie said, 'Well, I've read mine . . . thought 'e might wanna swap!'

At the Cross Keys I found Holmes sitting at a table in the bar parlour, a pewter pot in front of him and an expression of triumph on his face. Moreover, as he spoke to me there was a ring of optimism in his voice. 'Watson! So you have returned from your trip to the big city. I await your report with interest.' Despite his seeming thirst for information I had, as always, that lingering doubt that he might already know everything that I could tell him. I remembered still with a touch of resentment that experience on Dartmoor when he had used me as a pawn. As I related my adventures with Mr Quelch, my words seemed to gain Holmes's full attention, surprise and even astonishment in turns.

When I had told him all that had happened he asked if he might be permitted to see the juvenile publications to which I had alluded. I handed him *The Magnet* and *The*

Gem, almost apologetically. Yet I noticed that he glanced through them with great interest and asked, 'May I keep these to read at my leisure?' I naturally assented, though I quite failed to see how they could be helpful in the matter of Quelch's missing manuscript. Placing the distinctive-looking boys' papers aside, Holmes said, 'Your report, whilst not helpful in aiding the recovery of the manuscript yet, raises interesting points which make the whole matter more singular than I had thought.'

'I have discovered nothing that will help you, then?'

'In the matter of the recovery, no, for I have already recovered Mr Quelch's manuscript!'

'What?'

'Ah, you are surprised? Then let me relate that which has occurred during your absence. I decided to try and see if anything more could be deduced from that ransom demand written upon the blank portion of a page, provided by a certain sporting newspaper. You may remember that I had found that the paper had been rested on a serrated surface. As you know, Watson, no detail is too small to pay possible dividends. I examined that writing again with my lens and decided that it had been written with the paper resting on perhaps a trunk, or grained leather suit-case.'

I admit that I rather failed to see, at the time, how this fact could aid the veteran detective in his investigations. However, I did not interrupt and he continued, 'I enlisted the services of the head boy, Wingate, once more. I asked him where the boys' trunks and boxes were stored in term time. He took me to the box-room which is at the very top of the main school building, all but an attic really. The room is evidently never locked but Wingate volunteered the information that the apartment is regularly used by certain bad-hats among the boys who are inclined to go there to smoke or play nap for money.'

I interrupted, 'You think that the writer of that note to Quelch might have written it in the box-room, resting it on one of the trunks? But I fail to see . . .'

He snapped back at me, 'Ah yes, Watson, you fail to see . . . sometimes that which is important and right in front of your nose! I searched out the only trunk which had its locks secured. No schoolboy's box or trunk would need to be locked when empty. Obviously, Master Harold Skinner, whose name was painted on the particular trunk, did not wish it to be opened. But I did so, very easily, with my penknife. Inside, sure enough, I found a thick bundle of foolscap, bound in two directions with string and sealed with red wax.'

I gasped, 'Quelch's manuscript!'

'Undoubtedly, my dear Watson, and still bearing a title sheet, recognizable as such despite its torn portion. The manuscript is safely upstairs in my bedroom.'

'And young Skinner is definitely the culprit?'

'Without a doubt. You may remember that recent events had already placed him in my mind as a possible suspect? We knew of his debt of fifteen pounds owed to the rascal, Banks. The amount mentioned in that ransom note was fifteen pounds. How like a schoolboy to ask only for the amount required to get him out of trouble! A hardened criminal would have asked for more on principle.'

I asked, 'What shall be your next move, Holmes?'

He said, 'I shall order another tankard of ale. Will you join me, Watson? I will in fact do nothing until the morrow, for there may be other developments before then. I have enlisted the services of young Wingate to watch the sundial in the Cloisters at ten of the clock, to see if anyone appears. I have sworn him to secrecy regarding my recovery of the manuscript.'

As it happened there was soon to be a further development. Master Harold Skinner of the Greyfriars Remove appeared at about nine-thirty in his regular disguise. He was pale and drawn and as before we could scarcely fail to hear his converse with the bookmaker, Banks, even through the thick ante-room curtain.

'Well, young Skinner, where's my fifteen pun?'

'You shall have it tonight, later, just before closing time. I've come to tell you that so that you will not do anything like you have threatened!'

'Orl right, tonight it is . . . but if you ain't 'ere with the dibs you'll be for it, young shaver!'

Skinner passed us as he made his exit from the Cross Keys, oblivious to all save the fearful web that he had woven for himself. After the cad of the Remove had left, Holmes said, 'We have only to wait here until closing time. Skinner is undoubtedly on his way to the sundial, full of expectation that the money will be left there.'

I said the obvious, 'But he cannot leave the manuscript there, Holmes, because you have it!'

My friend replied, 'I doubt if Skinner knows that. He will visit the box-room and collect the remarkably similar bundle of blank foolscap sheets that I have left in his trunk, complete with a torn title sheet bearing my forgery of Quelch's writing. I have tied and sealed it in the same style. When he gets to the sundial, Wingate will grab him and take him to the headmaster. Should he elude Wingate he will turn up here before closing time to whine to Banks for mercy.'

I considered it all, 'So you mean that if he does not come here he will have been apprehended and the situation resolved?'

'Exactly, Watson, and that is what I expect to happen. Tomorrow we will have the pleasure of returning to Mr Quelch his precious manuscript.'

We waited until the public house closed and heard the last of its noisy patrons fade from earshot. Then Holmes said, 'Watson, obviously Wingate has caught Skinner in the act. I think I will turn in . . . possibly to sleep, but more likely to take the opportunity of reading *The Magnet* and *The Gem*!'

CHAPTER SEVEN

'Give a Dog a Bad Name'

On the following morning I was awoken at about half-past eight by Sherlock Holmes. He was fully dressed though unshaven and I remember musing that this was the very first time I had observed my friend other than clean of chin save of course when in disguise. Why, even on Dartmoor when he had surprised me in the stone-age-dwellers' hut in which he had been living, I had noted that he was as clean of chin and linen as if he had been still at Baker Street.

He fairly roared at me, 'Watson, stir yourself quickly, get dressed but do not trifle with niceties, we must go at once to Greyfriars!'

I noticed that he was hugging Quelch's sealed and bundled manuscript to him and that there was a bulge in his pea-jacket, as if from concealed papers. It took me but a couple of minutes to throw on my clothes during the whole

of which time Holmes breathed hard and tutted frequently
As we emerged from my room I was surprised to encounter
George Wingate, looking somewhat distraught. We ex-
changed polite nods, then, as we descended the stairs,
Holmes said to me, 'There has been a development which I
did not anticipate. We must lose no time in reaching the
school and, as we go, I will allow Wingate to tell you in his
own words what has occurred.' Then, as we entered the
lane making for the towpath, Holmes pointed a finger at
the Greyfriars head boy, in the style of a conductor bring-
ing an instrument into his orchestra. Obediently Wingate
began his story.

'Well, Doctor, last night I hid myself in the bushes near
the Cloisters sundial just as Mr Holmes had requested me
to. As we had earlier found the manuscript in Skinner's
trunk I was expecting that young rascal. But I had received
orders to grab anyone who appeared upon the scene. Those
were my exact terms of reference . . .'

Holmes interjected, 'I must learn to choose my words
more carefully!'

Wingate resumed, 'Imagine my surprise when punctu-
ally at ten-thirty, young Vernon-Smith appeared upon the
scene. As head boy of course I had no alternative but to
grab him and take him to Dr Locke. The Head was furious, for he had been listening to an orchestral piece on the
gramophone. He sent for Mr Quelch and the result was a
sort of on-the-spot kangaroo court, with Vernon-Smith
being sacked . . . that is, expelled. Not only that, but
flogged first in the Big Hall, in front of the whole school.'

I spluttered, 'And you said nothing, Wingate?'

He explained, 'How could I, having been sworn to
secrecy by Mr Holmes? Anyway, Quelch convinced Dr

Locke that his suspicions had been founded all along, telling him about the note concerning the appointment at the sundial and so on. Neither he nor the Head were likely to listen to me. In any case, it is hardly my place to question the decisions of my headmaster. Only Mr Holmes can do that!'

I asked, 'You could not send a message to us at the Cross Keys last night?'

He coloured slightly. 'As head boy I have to set an example and this would hardly include breaking bounds late at night and visiting a public house on an errand which I could not even divulge if apprehended, Dr Watson!'

I secretly thought that he might have risked it, but said nothing. By this time we had reached the school gates and Holmes, instead of echoing my mental chastisement of Wingate, demanded of him, 'Quickly, Wingate, lead us directly to the Big Hall!'

As we burst into that ancient and austere apartment we came upon a scene which was perhaps rare in an English public school, even at that time. It was one ugly enough to couple it in my mind with the long discontinued public execution of murderers. The whole school was assembled, sitting, facing a platform upon which the archaic punishment was to take place. There upon the platform stood, or rather crouched, Gosling the porter, bearing upon his broad back the hapless Vernon-Smith. Dr Locke, usually so benevolent of expression, was stern and pale faced. He grasped in his right hand the seldom-used birch. He held it poised, ready to deal the first blow upon the bare back of the luckless Bounder.

Sherlock Holmes wasted not a second in running down the centre aisle towards the platform and shouting 'Stop!'

in a voice that could not but be obeyed had it not resounded through the hall a fraction of a second too late to prevent the first blow from falling.

Swipe!

The cruel birch made violent contact with the young lad's back but produced from him no cry or answering sound. But the Bounder's face was contorted with pain, and the effort that he needed in order not to cry out. Dr Locke lowered the birch and glared down at the detective.

'Mr Holmes, what is the meaning of this intrusion?'

Sherlock Holmes clambered upon the platform and spoke in a loud, clear voice. 'Dr Locke, in attempting to prevent an injustice I have unfortunately been unable to prevent a portion of this unjust punishment from being carried out.'

'What do you mean, sir? Pray explain yourself!'

'I mean, sir, that Vernon-Smith is innocent of the charge which you and Mr Quelch have brought against him.'

The Head seemed almost apoplectic in his protestations. 'I would have you know, Mr Holmes, that I have proof of his guilt. I am, I trust, a just man. I would not expel and flog a boy who was innocent!'

Mr Quelch could contain himself no longer; jumping up from his seat upon the staff bench to say, 'Mr Holmes, like my headmaster I am, I hope, just. But I am convinced that this wretched boy is the culprit and deserving of the punishment that you, sir, have merely deferred!'

There was a silence throughout the great apartment of assembly, uncharacteristic of a gathering composed mainly of schoolboys. Among them I had noticed Skinner, who sat impassively, without a hint of colour in his ashen face. I knew that Holmes had noticed him too. The detective said, 'I have Mr Quelch's missing manuscript in my hands at this very moment and I am in a position to name the real culprit. Certainly he is *not* Master Vernon-Smith! However, I suggest that you give the rascal an opportunity to own up, in the true Greyfriars way. Some hint of leniency might encourage the culprit to step forward.'

Mr Quelch had been too engrossed in other matters to notice previously the bundle which Holmes held. His eyes gleamed and his expression changed from triumph at the thought of regaining his precious bundle of foolscap to the uncertainty as to why the arch-Baker Street detective did not at once hand it to him.

He said, 'Mr Holmes, I am grateful to you for regaining my *History of Greyfriars* for me. I will express my appreciation to you in private, later. Now if I may have my manuscript?'

The school-master extended two bony hands to take that which was his. There was desperation mixed with a touch of avarice in the action. Holmes, to my faint surprise and Quelch's anger, clutched the bundle closer to him. He said, 'Mr Quelch, we are in the midst of a situation in which you are yourself involved, indicating injustice. Please have the goodness to be patient in regard to the matter of the return of your writings. We have much to discuss, a little later. At this moment, even more important matters are under review.'

I could see that Quelch was furious now. He shook his head about in a most stork-like manner and said, 'My dear sir, the manuscript which you hold is mine! You were hired to recover it for me. Obviously you have done so and I am grateful, but please give it to me at once!'

Holmes seemed neither offended nor angry, but replied in a measured and reasonable tone, saying, 'Mr Quelch, far from being hired, as you so delicately call it, and which would not have been possible as I am retired, in truth I came here as a favour to my old friend Dr Watson. He in turn had become involved through a plea for help from his old headmaster, which as an old head boy he could hardly refuse. Do you really wish me to say to you that which I had reserved to express in private, here upon this platform? If so, I will be happy to do so and to return your manuscript in public!'

Quelch looked long and hard at Holmes and seemed to read in his eyes that he would be better off being patient. He breathed heavily and then said, 'Very well, Mr Holmes. Of course I am beholden to you and will proceed as you wish.' Then he turned to Dr Locke and said, 'My apologies, Headmaster. I have interrupted important matters through anxiety concerning my own affairs.'

As for Dr Locke, he had calmed considerably. He said, 'Mr Holmes, if what you say is true I am appalled at my own mistake and will give the real culprit a chance to own up and put this matter right. As for leniency, well if he does own up I will not send him away from Greyfriars. But he will receive the flogging that he deserves! I will give the rascal one minute to speak. Otherwise, expulsion must be added to the punishment.'

Holmes caught Skinner's eye and inclined his head slightly, as if to say, 'You can be flogged or expelled *and* flogged, the choice is yours.'

After a painful silence of only a few seconds, Harold Skinner rose from his seat on the Remove benches and walked unsteadily to the platform. He raised a hand and said, 'Please, Dr Locke, sir, it was I who took the manuscript. I only did it for a lark, but I'm willing to face the music now . . . I didn't intend for Smithy to take my medicine.'

'Very well, Skinner. As you have owned up I will not send you away, but I shall flog you with the utmost severity!' The headmaster spoke severely, then turned to the Porter and said, 'Gosling, lower Vernon-Smith and take up Skinner.'

The Bounder, having replaced his shirt, collar, tie and jacket, was relieved to rejoin his school fellows on the Remove benches. Not unnaturally, he grinned cynically as Skinner was divested of his shirt and taken up upon Gosling's back.

Whack . . . whack . . . whack!

'Ow . . . ow . . . stoppit!'

The helpless Skinner writhed and screamed.

Whack . . . whack . . . whack!

Three more heavy blows descended and then Skinner was lowered and allowed to dress and return to the Remove benches. He did all this with the uppermost difficulty. Of course though even a dreadful cad like Skinner did not blub in public, it was clear that he was near to it.

Dr Locke discarded his birch with relief, then turned his attention to the Remove benches, but his target was Vernon-Smith and not Skinner this time. He spoke in severe tones, 'Vernon-Smith, why were you in the Cloisters at that time of night when you should have been in your dormitory?'

The Bounder shrugged and then said, 'Fact is, I'd been to the races at Wapshot, sir, lost all my tin on the jolly old gee-gees and had to walk back. The Cloisters was a short cut to the drainpipe that I had to climb to get back into the jolly old dorm!'

Dr Locke was horrified. 'Upon my word! Why did you not tell me this last night?'

'Well, sir, I didn't think you would believe me. But now that the jolly old detective johnny has explained, perhaps you will? Oh, and I hope you'll also believe that I had nothing to do with old Quelch's manuscript!'

The Head breathed long and hard and then said, 'Vernon-Smith, due to my action which bordered upon injustice I will say no more about your breaking of bounds or the insolent way in which you have referred to your form-master. I had intended to apologize to you for what has occurred, but I no longer feel bound to do so as you have only your own foolish, reckless and rebellious behaviour to blame for what has happened.'

Vernon-Smith said, 'Yes sir, thank you, sir!' He was as insolent as ever and all but winked at Holmes and me.

Dr Locke dismissed the assembly and there was a buzz of excited boyish conversation as the pupils and staff filed out of the Big Hall. To be sure, the drama they had witnessed would be the main topic of Greyfriars conversation for many a day to come. Holmes held aloft the manuscript and spoke rather sharply to the Remove master. 'Mr Quelch, you have been patient and I believe we can now deal with the matter of your *History of Greyfriars* But, as I have already suggested, it should be in private.' For a few seconds it seemed as if Quelch might repeat his earlier behaviour. But sanity prevailed and he said, 'Mr Holmes, I will be happy to receive Dr Watson and yourself in my study in half-an-hour's time.' He bowed, for now he had completely regained his composure and departed with a swish of his gown which had a certain theatricality.

The Greyfriars boys had been remarkably silent throughout the proceedings, but now their shrill young voices were given as much freedom as their owners thought they could get away with. There were cries of 'Good old Smithy' and 'Scrag that cad Skinner'! But as it happened, Skinner was too pitiful after his flogging and even the worst bully could not bring himself to lay hands on the pale, drawn youth as he retreated to lick his wounds. He had, however, been fortunate not to have been expelled, so we did not waste sympathy on him. As for the Bounder, he was cheered and carried shoulder-high out into the quad. The prefects and even the masters had the sense not to interfere with this demonstration of healthy high spirits. Many of the juniors gathered around Holmes to express their feelings.

'I say, Mr Holmes, congratters!'

'Rather, hear, hear!'

'The congratterfulness is terrific, honoured and esteemed sahib!'

Peter Todd said, 'You rest your jolly old case, sir, what?'

Even the sedate Wingate said, 'Jolly well done, sir. All's well that ends well, what?'

After Holmes had shaken hands with at least two dozen boys and masters we returned to the platform where Dr Locke sat alone. He said, 'My dear Holmes, I am so grateful that you managed to prevent the worst of the injustice that I was about to administer. I blame myself for what happened.'

I said, 'Come, sir, to err is human and I know that justice is strong in you.'

As we left the hall we all but collided with the substantial figure of Joe Banks. As recognition dawned in him he backed away and flinched as if expecting the pugilism of a night or two before to break out again. He said, '"Ere, you keep orf!' But Holmes reassured him, 'Pray calm yourself, Mr Banks. I have no wish to exchange blows with you, I never had, the idea was entirely your own. But I do wish to discuss a certain matter with you as we leave.' The unsavoury one started, but regaining a little of his courage said, 'Leave . . . 'Oo said anyfink abaht leaving? I gotta see the 'ead teacher. Young Skinner owes me fifteen pun, 'e just h'aint paid up. I gotta see abaht it and it h'aint no concern of yourn!'

Holmes warned, 'I intend to make it my business if you insist on raising the matter. If you speak to Dr Locke about Master Skinner and his so-called debt, I in turn will be forced to visit my friend Inspector Grimes. He might be rather interested in your recent activities.'

I added, 'Off-course betting is illegal, as is the use of licensed premises for gambling!'

Banks looked startled, 'Grimey, the rozzers . . . 'ere, what's your game?'

Holmes spoke with clarity and sincerity. 'My game, sir, is to prevent an unscrupulous rascal like yourself from taking advantage of a foolish, weak and impressionable boy. Consider Skinner's debt paid or deal with me. If you want another boxing lesson I'll be happy to oblige. By the way, my name is Sherlock Holmes!'

The beery bookie was taken aback and decided to take the hint and walked away, muttering, ''Ow's a cove to earn a living?'

Our unwashed and unshaven condition was causing Holmes and I enough embarrassment to make us glad to take advantage of Wingate's suggestion that we use the sixth-form bathroom. He said, 'The whole school will be in chapel so you will not be disturbed. I have borrowed some razors from one of the masters and you will find soap and clean towels.'

The large old-fashioned bathroom was of a spartan kind, considered suitable for senior schoolboys, but its facilities were more than welcome to us. Indeed, soon we were presentable enough to keep our appointment, although well short of immaculate! We made our way towards the masters' studies and we could hear the school choir's rendition of a stirring hymn. We found the precincts of the school unusually deserted, for Chapel on a Sunday morning was compulsory for masters and boys alike. Doubtless, Mr Quelch had needed to ask special permission from the headmaster to be able to keep our appointment. We knocked upon the now familiar oak door and entered as the equally familiar acid-toned voice bade us to do so.

'Pray be seated, gentlemen . . . I believe you have good tidings?' Quelch even attempted a crusty smile when Holmes placed the tied bundle of foolscap upon his desk. 'Ah yes, as you had intimated, it is my *History of Greyfriars*, or rather its first instalment.'

Holmes looked enigmatically at Quelch as he enquired, 'Are you not going to unfasten the bundle at least to make sure that all the pages are there? In fact, perhaps I may help you to do so?' Holmes made a half-hearted movement with his right hand in the direction of the manuscript.

'No! That is . . . thank you, but no . . . I can see that the seals are intact.' Quelch had uttered the word 'No' with a surprising urgency even if his following words had been more controlled. His behaviour had, I felt, bordered upon gross ingratitude. There had been no 'Thank you' even, for the return of those writings which he had considered so precious. I felt compelled to say, 'Mr Quelch, I feel sure that my friend has only your best interests at heart. His words and actions are and have ever been prompted by the best of motives.'

Quelch had, I felt, taken on the air of a trapped man. But why? He had his manuscript and despite his somewhat puzzling behaviour when I had observed him in London I had expected some display of gratitude on his part. Surely the man had nothing to fear? I wondered if I had spoken more warmly than I had intended. He had looked very sharply at me as I spoke, but now he relaxed his hatchet features into some sort of accepted idea of benevolence. He spoke with as little acidity as I believe he was able to. 'Yes, Dr Watson, you are quite right to chastise me, for I have indeed been guilty of ingratitude. Mr Holmes, please excuse my rudeness and put it down to the strain of almost losing my life's work. But for you, my dear sir, I might well have lost it!'

Holmes's next words were puzzling as far as I was concerned. He said, 'Not just the work of a week or at most a month, then, Mr Richards . . . or should I call you Mr Hamilton, or Mr Clifford, or maybe Mr Conquest?'

At Holmes's words the school-master rose sharply from his chair. I was myself startled at Holmes's words too, especially as he had used those several names that I had heard before used by a very eccentric Fleet Street editor.

Quelch said, hesitatingly, 'Why . . . why do you call me by those names, Mr Holmes? My name is Quelch, Henry Samuel Quelch, as you are so well aware.'

Holmes replied, 'Oh, I'm sure that Quelch is your real name, as you say . . .'

'Then . . . then why?'

The detective withdrew from inside his jacket a bundle of what appeared to be those juvenile publications which I had handed him on the previous evening. He did this with a dramatic, theatrical gesture. I could not contain my own amazed curiosity, asking, 'Holmes, why have you brought those childish papers here?'

He answered, 'Not so childish really, Watson. You see, unlike yourself I have actually read every word of these journals, last night. They are in fact extremely well written. The styles of Messrs Richards, Clifford and Conquest are all but identical, leading me to believe that they are pen names for a single writer. If this is so, he has a formidable output. Moreover, there is a realism of dialogue and character which rings a note of familiarity.'

I failed to completely follow his meaning and said as much. He replied, 'Very well, Watson, allow me to read aloud a few paragraphs from the leading story in *The Gem*, that is, if Mr Quelch will allow me to do so?'

Quelch shrugged his permission and Holmes began. A superb actor, I have always believed Holmes is a great loss to the London stage. He gave that excerpt all the vocal roundness of an Irving or Gillette. Moreover, his gift for mimicry made me believe that I recognized all the characters . . .

'I say, you chaps, look here, no larks!'

Baggy Trimble, the fattest junior at St Jim's School, looked warily at the four fellows as they strode determinedly towards him.

'Ah, there you are, you fat brigand. I'll teach you to snaffle my hamper!'

It was Tom Merry who spoke, usually of sunny disposition as his name suggested, yet presently extremely angry. He and his chums had looked forward to sampling the contents of the hamper, but on entering the study they found that the contents had been rifled.

'I – I – say, warrer you all walking towards me for? I never had your tuck you know. You can ask Levison . . . I never gave him a cake to keep quiet about it . . . nothing of the sort, old chaps. I wouldn't do such a thing. The thought of snaffling a fellow's tuck would never enter my head. It must have been Figgins, I saw him hanging around when I was opening the hamper. Not that I did open it . . . oh crikey!'

Before Trimble could incriminate himself further and receive his just punishment he was reprieved by the appearance of Mr Ratcliffe, his form-master. The 'fiscal four' politely greeted their form-master and left the scene. Ratcliffe looked at the laziest member of his form and said, 'Trimble, you are a disgrace! Your clothing and features appear to carry traces of some sort of comestibles.'

'Oh no, sir, scarcely a morsel of food has passed my lips today. If anyone has been telling whoppers about my having snaffled their tuck I shouldn't take any notice of them, sir, if I were you. I never went into Merry's study when he was playing footer and I certainly never touched his hamper. In fact I never even knew that Merry had a hamper.' He trailed off uneasily . . . 'H – has he got a hamper, sir?'

Mr Ratcliffe breathed hard. He said, 'Upon my word, Trimble, you are the most foolish, lazy and greedy boy that I have ever encountered.'

As Holmes tossed the periodical onto the desk, Quelch's face was an ashen mask.

In sheer amazement, I said, 'But it's Bunter . . . and Cherry . . . and you, Mr Quelch!'

There was a long silence, broken eventually by Quelch himself. He said, ruefully, 'So, Mr Holmes, you have discovered my secret. I cannot deny that I am the author of that juvenile story, an excerpt from which you have just read aloud. For some years now I have been writing boys' stories under a variety of noms-de-plume: Frank Richards, Owen Conquest, Martin Clifford, Ralph Redway, and there are others. But I can assure you that Henry Samuel Quelch is my real name, although I have told my publishers that I am one Charles Hamilton. They have no address for me. I take all manuscripts to them in person. I journey to Fleet Street each Saturday afternoon to deliver my writings. It would not have done at all for Dr Locke to know of my little side-line, for although what I do is perfectly lawful it would strike him as an undignified occupation for a member of his staff. I started in a small way and through the years it has grown, although now it takes every moment of my spare time to keep up my output.'

Holmes said, 'Your preoccupation with your *History of Greyfriars*, though, legitimizes your writing activity?'

'Exactly. My manuscripts are always disguised, as is the one on my desk. This is to prevent prying eyes discovering my preoccupation with Baggy Trimble, Tom Merry and the rest.'

I enquired, 'Your characters, dialogue and story-plots. These are inspired perhaps by the school life around you?'

Quelch nodded. 'Quite so, and were I required to resign my position to devote myself to writing full-time I would be denied this rich vein of inspiration.'

Holmes chuckled. 'Mr Quelch, were I wearing a hat I would doff it to you! I suppose the manuscript on the desk is anxiously awaited in Fleet Street?'

'Oh yes, it is a novella of some thirty thousand words, the first of a series that I am to supply for a new monthly boys' periodical. It took me a long time to write, for me, and would have taken almost as long to replace. The publisher was pressing me for it, which is why I was so anxious to regain it. But none of this is of importance now.'

Holmes asked sharply, 'Why not?'

Quelch bowed his head as he said, 'Well I feel sure that you will find it necessary to inform Dr Locke of my extra-curricular activities.'

My friend all but snapped back, 'Nonsense! Why should I tell him? What you are doing is not only lawful, but productive of my admiration. I am a public-school man myself, Mr Quelch, so I am not a sneak!'

The colour began to return to Quelch's cheeks. He looked enquiringly at me. I answered his glance with the words, 'I see no reason to inform the good doctor of such a very minor indiscretion, sir!'

The Remove master looked from one to the other of us and said, 'Gentlemen, I am so much in your debt.' I tried to lighten the mood further by saying, 'I trust that Holmes and I will eventually become characters in *The Magnet* or *The Gem*?'

That which I had intended as a joke, Quelch took quite seriously. He said, 'Well, Doctor, I already have some notes upon a character partially inspired by Sherlock Holmes. I think I might call him Ferrers Locke and domicile him in Baker Street, with a young ex-public-schoolboy as his Watson!'

Outside the school buildings we encountered a familiar stout figure rolling towards us. He said, 'I say, Mr Holmes, have you found old Quelch's scribblings yet?'

I felt that my friend was extremely tolerant of the foolish fat boy. He replied, 'Yes, Master Bunter, all is well now and Mr Quelch's *History of Greyfriars* is safely back in his hands.' Bunter seemed relieved and said, 'Oh good, because he's been jolly waxy about it, you know. We might get a bit of peace now.' Then, as we strolled towards the school gates, Bunter called after us, 'I say, don't walk away while a chap is talking. I wanted to tell you that I've been disappointed about a postal order . . . I say . . . stop! Beasts!' Bunter got tired of having to walk quite so fast.

At the gates we came upon Herbert Vernon-Smith, who smiled at us and insisted upon shaking us both by the hand. Then he said, 'Mr Holmes, I want to thank you for saving me from the jolly old sack! You too, Doctor, you played your part. Just think when you first came here I thought you were a pair of stuffy old duffers. But I was wrong, I apologize.' We accepted this back-handed compliment as graciously as we felt able.

Walking along the towpath beside the gleaming, silvery and fast-moving Sark I remarked to Holmes upon the singularity of an elderly school-master being the author of boy's fiction. He said, 'Oh, I don't know, Watson. I mean, who would imagine a respectable doctor to be a consulting detective's Boswell?'

Epilogue at Fowlhaven

About three months after the episode of Mr Quelch's missing *History of Greyfriars* I visited Holmes again at Fowlhaven. As we sat in his cool parlour with its antique beams and chalk-white ceiling I noticed with nostalgic pleasure that he still possessed his scrapbooks, memorabilia and monographs, not to mention the portrait of her late Majesty. The Turkish slipper still kept his tobacco fresh.

'My dear Watson, how very nice to see you again. Though I do trust that you are not here upon an errand for Scotland Yard, or . . .' his steely eyes twinkled, 'Dr Locke of your old school?'

I laughed, 'Nothing so dramatic, just a desire to see an old friend, and give him this!'

I cast upon the table a copy of *The Gem*. On its buff cover was a depiction of a boy, bare to the waist, hoisted upon the back of a hefty character remindful of Gosling, receiving a flogging from a mild enough looking figure in mortarboard and gown, wielding a birch. In the foreground of the picture a lean figure with a prominent aquiline nose, raising a commanding right hand. Beneath the picture was printed the single word: 'Stop!' Above the cartoon and beneath the paper's title were the words 'Saved by the sleuth!' In smaller lettering below it read: 'Ferrers Locke and his boy assistant save Levison from the sack!'

Holmes took up the paper with interest and was soon sitting in his armchair completely absorbed. He is without doubt the swiftest reader that I have ever encountered and in perhaps twenty minutes he had absorbed all of the twenty thousand or more words of the story. Then he asked me, 'You have read it, of course?'

I replied, 'Every word, and I think old Quelch has got rather a nerve!'

Sherlock Holmes said, 'Oh, I don't know, Watson. It's rather amusing really and the character modelled upon myself is quite interesting. I see he has turned you into a sixteen-year-old youth, and Vernon-Smith has become Levison. There is no suggestion whatever that Mr Ratcliffe is a secret writer of schoolboy fiction. But good old Baggy Trimble is still raiding tuck boxes and borrowing against the arrival of a postal order!'

I admitted to Holmes that in my old age I had become a regular reader of the stories of Messrs Richards, Clifford, Conquest and Redway. But, as I remarked, 'Although the interest at first was through knowing that Mr Quelch had written them, I have stayed a regular reader simply because they are rattling good school-yarns.'

Holmes agreed, adding, 'Not only is his output near to impossible but the quality of his work is superb, far above that of the periodicals for which he writes. He is without doubt, Watson, the schoolboy's Dickens!'